MW00379925

# Lost in Wyoming

Also by Scott Sadil

*Cast from the Edge: Tales of an Uncommon Fly Fisher*

*Angling Baja: One Man's Fly Fishing Journey Through the Surf*

# Lost in Wyoming

*stories*

## Scott Sadil

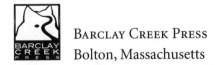

BARCLAY CREEK PRESS
Bolton, Massachusetts

*Lost in Wyoming: Stories*

ISBN–13: 978–1–936008–00–1
ISBN–10: 1–936008–00–9

Barclay Creek Press, LLC
PO Box 249
Bolton, MA 01740–0249 USA

www.barclaycreek.com

Publisher: James D. Anker
Page design: Dutton & Sherman Design
Jacket design: Dutton & Sherman Design
Jacket photo: A river near Jenny Lake in Grand Teton National Park,
    © Shutterstock Images LLC
Author photo: Carol Sternkopf

For my sons, Riley and Patrick, with love.

❧

My deepest gratitude for responses and advice
from the following readers:

Pete Fromm, Althea Hukari, Susan Hess,
Keith Liggett, David Melody, Nan Noteboom,
Kerry Reuff, Barb Schuppe, and Ellen Waterston.

# contents

I've spent as much of my life fishing as decency allowed,
and sometimes I don't let even that get in my way.
—*Thomas McGuane*

Perhaps no one is who he seems to be.
—*Jim Harrison*

*one*

# Lost in Wyoming

A sprinkler somewhere produces the sound of rain against the taut skin of Aaron Packard's two-man tent. Or his ex-wife's tent, as he thinks of it even now, worming his summer bag free of the ripstop walls, trying not to disturb Elaine, his new girlfriend. Agitated, he runs a bare arm through the confusion of nylon, searching for signs of dampness; at the same time, the approach and retreat of falling water offers relief from the close interior. Outside, Packard imagines, the campground dust settles beneath each moistening sweep, and tiny breaths of evaporation cool the warm, Wyoming night.

Roused from sleep, Packard reconsiders the course of his probing hand. But there are reasons he and Elaine aren't sharing the same bag. Bedding down, she blamed the heat—an excuse he now finds so lame he feels certain a woman her age could not have possibly used it had there been a trace of light in the little tent to reveal one another's experienced eyes. He would like to resolve these differences soon. Beside him, this healthy, handsome, independent woman remains silent beneath the rise and fall of patter across the tent's domed surface, her entire body encased—despite the heat—in the cocoon of her sleeping bag. Packard, in the ease of his thoughts, permits himself a certain smugness: Now seems as good a time as any.

Still, he hesitates. Think what he might, he's afraid of . . . . *blowing it.* He considers again the tent's wet exterior—and he envisions the frailty of such porous membranes against the lightest touch, much less the pressures of genuine passion. Later, he will come to recognize deeper sources of his concerns: It would have been just like his ex-wife, astride him in a leaky tent, to come unglued.

Stalled by history and doubt, Packard hears the sprinklers shut down. Rivulets of water, inches from his head, meld with the sound of the river rising through the sudden, midnight calm. *Of course they'll stay dry.* He recalls his ex-wife's pride in spending top dollar, a tendency he had ceased to dispute long before she attached her hopes to the intimacies of backcountry travel, a plan from which he was immediately excluded. He tries to remember just what went wrong, how he had failed her that time, too. "Anxiety attack," she announced, slamming the doors of her Subaru, after her one and only overnight trip with their then eight-year-old son. "I was awake the entire night"—and somehow he was to blame, he was sure, though he never concluded if her dark night rose from visions of bear, rutting elk, or an extraterrestrial axe murderer.

Packard rolls over, aiming his body to conform to Elaine's shrouded back. And at that instant a sound as if an amplified rattlesnake, or the discharge of automatic weaponry, erupts from the far side of the tent. Elaine jolts half upright, a cat-like peal rising in her throat. Packard throws an arm around her—and his hand is immediately showered by spray leaping off the inside of the tent from a sprinkler head just outside.

2

"Jesus effing Christ!" shouts Elaine, and in her haste to remove herself from the trail of water, she practically smothers Packard with invective and spontaneous nudity.

"Out of my way!" she finishes, her bottom receding from view through the tent's doorway—a kind of visual echo, notes Packard, to the intensity of the shrieking zipper the moment her bare flesh grazed his upturned face.

In his van, they rummage through duffel bags and find towels, dry clothes. Seated on the passenger bench, Elaine dresses while Packard, having politely removed himself, hangs their wet sleeping bags over the open side doors. Then he goes to the back and begins unloading fishing gear—waders and boots, rod tubes, his Sterilite fly-tying bins—making room for the two of them. But when he finishes, Packard finds Elaine curled up in his Woolrich travel blanket, on the bench seat fast asleep.

◯

A week ago, entering Wyoming, Packard felt everything was going just fine.

Granted, this marked their first trip together, a dicey enterprise for both of them. Elaine, a grandmother twice over, from two different marriages, taught art at the same high school where Packard taught history. Twice he had agreed to take her brother, vacationing from California, fishing on the Deschutes; after the first outing, Elaine asked Packard to tie her brother a half-dozen steelhead flies, which she arranged on cork pedestals glued to the bottom of a lidded Van Gogh stationery box and mailed south for Christmas. The following winter, she presented Packard with an exacting pencil sketch of Clint Eastwood, drawn from an eerie black-and-white magazine photo taken during the filming of *Unforgiven*. On another occasion, she claimed that Packard also reminded her of Keith Richards; on another, Jack Nicholson—not, of course, she added, when these stars

3

were young, but as the shameless, gray-haired old men seen in the likes of *People* magazine today.

None of this meant much to Packard. He and Elaine belonged to a staff of over seventy-five teachers, most of them with public faces and discreet private lives, neither of which intersected except for those sad cases who seemed, in effect, to have never left high school and all its fabulous drama. Packard felt nothing toward Elaine but collegial goodwill—not until Elaine's third marriage collapsed, when her husband of two years, an economics instructor at the community college, fell in love online and, shortly thereafter, rediscovered Jesus.

He learned the highlights of her betrayal at the start of the new school year, when Elaine began visiting his classroom to ask his advice about salmon fishing. He had little to offer. Embracing her sudden independence, Elaine, along with a cousin from across the river, assembled spinners on her kitchen table and took up casting for fall chinook from the busy rocks below the Klickitat gorge, a style of fishing Packard all but ignored. Yet he shared in her enthusiasm, imagining her perched above the frothy current, skirting the attentions of the rough, intemperate crowd, glimpsed each afternoon as Packard himself headed up river, searching for steelhead with flies and a two-handed rod.

On a Saturday in late October, when she finally hooked and landed a fish, Elaine phoned Packard, wondering what she should do now.

"Did you kill it yourself?" he asked, following her through her kitchen with his knives, carborundum, and Arkansas stone.

"The guy who netted it for me did." Elaine, in T-shirt and pink shorts, appeared fresh from a shower. She moved aside as they stepped out onto the back deck, allowing Packard to see the fish, yet remaining nearby, as if to remind him that no matter what he did to it, it still belonged to her. "He got a big stick and whacked it on the head."

Stiff as cardboard, the dead salmon, lying in shade atop the picnic table, shared the gray cast of dead fish everywhere. Packard guessed it at twenty, twenty-two pounds. But what did he know? he asked himself, trying to recall the last fish this size he had actually ever weighed—a thought that lifted the corners of his mouth as he pictured Elaine, hovering beside him, engaged in inelegant struggle, trying to stop a running salmon compelled by timeless desire.

"A priest," he said.

Elaine turned her face to his—and in the green of her eyes he saw the curiosity, and need to discover, that foretold for him as much about a woman as he was sure he would ever know.

"I don't think so," she said, holding his gaze. "The guy smelled like beer and cussed a blue streak."

"No, not the guy." Packard shook his head and began scrubbing a burr into the blade of one of his knives. "That's what you call a stick like that. A priest. For administering last rites. Your gillie carries one."

"*Gillie?*"

He taught her to fly cast during winter. Her clever painter hands found inventive ways to mishandle the rod, yet her errors fell away quickly, leaving behind a compact stroke unblemished by bad habits. More than once Packard wondered if she might have a knack for this. She insisted on paying for her own equipment, a show of independence Packard honored by presenting her with a fly box filled with his favorite trout patterns, an act of generosity unmatched since his two sons finished college and married, absorbed by lives of their own.

They were miles up the Yakima canyon, aimed at trout over spring break, when Elaine took the fly box from Packard's outstretched hand. He kept his eyes on the road. He hadn't wrapped the box, hadn't paid top dollar for one, hadn't imagined that kind of thing would matter. Now he wasn't sure. What he had thought about while tying the flies, he recalled, steering through patches of sunlit rain, was that she needed flies and these would work; and if she didn't have her own, and plenty of them, she wouldn't be on her own—and that was the absolute worst way to take anyone fishing who you think might really want to give the sport a try.

Now he hoped she'd like them, too.

By the time they reached the bridge at Umtanum, Elaine had removed, one at a time, a half-dozen different flies, asking Packard to describe what each one was made of, what it imitated, how she would know when to fish it. He rejected the dour notion she might be humoring him. They padded across the suspended timbers in a chill, persistent mist, their felts leaving rows of greasy footprints that seemed to Packard to melt into the treads themselves when he turned to check the horizon to the east.

"This stuff's going to hold," he said, gesturing with his rod tip to indicate the low clouds, the drizzle, the dense, midday calm.

"And that's *good*?" Elaine looked at him from inside her Gore-Tex, her chin tucked well below her neck.

"Better," said Packard, stopping at the far end of the bridge. He peered down along the upstream bank. "Check it out."

Rising fish left tangles of nervous welts riding the even rain-splattered current, the trout exposing themselves here and there in the kind of lazy feeding that suggested to Packard a meal of profound dimensions. Blue-winged olives, he thought—which he had antici-pated, pointing out for Elaine the row of Little Olive Flymphs when she stood, back at the van, peering into her brand-new box of flies.

"We can catch these?" she now asked, close to Packard as they both leaned over the handrail, looking down at the dark, blemished water.

"We shall see," he allowed.

6

They did. For Elaine, it was the first time she had ever found herself in such a furious concentration of sport, and she comported herself—given Packard's help—with equal measures of artistic resolve and fitful, irrational shrieking. Packard, although an old hand, descended into his own blend of practiced execution and only partially repressed hysteria, a result of his deep understanding of the rarity, in the long run, of these profligate occasions. After one particularly energetic fish, one that had seemed inclined, at the start, to empty Packard's little wailing reel, he found himself down on his knees at water's edge, a position from which he thrust his index finger toward Elaine's amused, mist-streaked gaze.

"Just like Wyoming!" he barked.

"*Wyoming?*"

That night, beside their campfire, exchanging sips with Elaine from his flask of Black Label, Packard returned to the subject, one of his favorite. Wyoming, he said, glancing up at the clearing nighttime sky, remained for him a kind of promised land, a place he could get lost in each summer fishing for trout in waters that retained, here and there, that flavor of Wild West fly fishing that seemed all but bred out of the sport. But Elaine cut him short. She had seen plenty of Wyoming in her day, too. Raised, she revealed, in Lemmon, South Dakota, she had crisscrossed Wyoming in her own restless search for something bigger than herself, an erratic, circuitous journey that had left in its wake the customary trail of broken promises, lost hopes, abandoned dreams—the palette of youth, she called it, that she turned her back on when she finally moved to Oregon, embraced art, and found work in the public schools.

Still, Elaine said, she had fond memories of Wyoming, too. And as the night advanced, she offered up glimpses of those good times, stories that seemed to Packard to be fueled by more than the afternoon's potent fishing or the lifting of spirits from his flask. Over dying flames and radiant midnight embers, Elaine unraveled an elaborate

7

tale that ended with a high-stakes game of eight ball in a roadhouse west of Casper. As her opponent, the lead singer of The Ghost Rats, the Saturday night band, stretched across the table, prepared to drop the decisive ball in the side pocket, Elaine raised her sweater over her head, and she rested her naked breasts on the felted cushions on opposite sides of the target.

Elaine held out the flask. Packard took it, studying her eyes in the fading firelight.

"Did he make it?"

Elaine looked back at him—and he thought, for a moment, he heard air pass between her teeth.

"That's not the point of the story," she said—and then she gave him a new look, a serious look, a glance that reminded Packard of how a big trout can sip a fly, delicate as that, and in the same instant you feel the weight of the fish all the way down to your kneecaps.

Packard awakes in a state of disorientation. The furious groan of a lone semi, pulling up the highway grade, has pitched the final, unrecalled moments of his dreams into a crescendo of confusion, leaving his heart racing. Through the van's open rear doors, he gazes into the incongruity of two dozen bighorn sheep grazing placidly amidst the picnic tables and blackened oil drum fire rings of empty campsites directly beyond the gravel Loop A roadway. The van itself seems to hum with the white noise of moving water—so that, even as his heart settles, Packard can't quite discern where exactly the river lies, nor what to do about the quiet breathing rising from the bench seat of the van.

He would like to call Elaine's attention to the outlandish roadside wildlife. More than this, however, he would like to present himself to the intimate confines of her private sleeping station. He feels confident that close proximity would resolve any significant differences that might still remain between them. He believes, in his heart, that come what may, there is room on that wide deep seat for both of them and all of their unfathomable needs and desires.

Yet Packard remains prone, anchored to the Therm-a-Rest pad spread along the length of the van's bare metal floor. The sheep drift off, puffs of condensation rising from their flaring nostrils, their delicate mouths pinching the freshly irrigated grass. To Packard it seems as if the herd as a whole answers to some power as pure as gravity, the herd's movement as much tidal, even astronomical, as it is in response to the inclinations of life, the needs of biology, the eloquent precepts of chemistry. Wrapped inside his tattered surplus Navy blanket, he recalls the years of dangerous dawns spent navigating his ex-wife's perilous moods, his touch or mere gesture igniting eruptions fueled by night-old wine, insomnia, and her endless hours of undisturbed attention spent burnishing his infinite capacity to fail her.

No, he will let Elaine sleep, he thinks, sitting up to reach for his fleece watchman's cap. He rustles through the outfall of last night's confused retreat. Dressed, he swings his legs out the back of the van.

"Honey?"

Above the seat, Elaine's hand reminds Packard of a prairie dog.

"Will you wake me when the coffee's ready?"

The inside of the tent looks like a wading pool. Standing water traces the lip of the bathtub-style floor, Elaine's wool socks floating in a corner as if a pair of mistreated whitefish. Packard pulls stakes and lifts an edge of the tent, spilling water out of the door while noticing the precise angle of the old Rainbird positioned just high enough to clear the coated taffeta flooring yet miss the eave of the rain fly, directly above where Elaine set to rest her pretty head.

How had he failed to spot this potential hazard the evening before? He acknowledges he might well have had other things on his mind. Packard carries the tent by its arched poles into warm sunlight flooding the gravel drive, recalling their first morning in the state, only a week ago, when he woke to find the lower walls of the tent girdled with a broad band of ice, a strip of frozen condensation that looked much the same as a stain of dried sweat discoloring the edge of a cap. No doubt, he reflects uneasily, things grew hot and heavy in the keen excitement that had seemed to build from the very moment they entered Wyoming—and which, by the time they finished fishing over an exquisite hatch of Pale Morning Duns their first afternoon on Hams Fork, left them fumbling, eventually, like teenagers in the nadir of his ex-wife's tent.

Packard leaves the tent open to dry and secures it as best he can on the hard-packed drive, working the light wire stakes at two corners down through the coarse gravel with his bare hands. The sun presses firmly on his back, promising another fierce day. They'll need to be on the water soon, before the heat consumes the cool of the canyon floor, engulfing the great boulders and naked rock walls, while the big browns recede with the retreating shadows.

But maybe that's just as well, he thinks, stabbing his thumb against the fuel tank of his old Coleman stove. He hears Elaine stirring but keeps his back to her, allowing her what little privacy she can find behind the sleeping bags draped over the open side doors. He recalls the grim moment the second day on Hams Fork after Elaine hooked what appeared to be a genuinely big fish, a heavy rainbow that showed itself once and then headed directly for the half-submerged cab of an old pickup truck the rancher of the property had tried to use as riprap to shore up an eroding bank. She never stood a chance. The trout got on the far side of the cab and sheared off the leader in a heartbeat. Then Elaine turned on him, her small pert body suddenly tense as a terrier's, her green eyes hurt, offended, furious, outraged—he couldn't tell which. Packard threw up his hands and offered an exaggerated shrug of his shoulders, trying to make light of the moment.

"Big ol' pig went right inside that Chevy and slammed the door."

But Elaine wouldn't hear a word of it. And that night, when he tried to start up where they had left off the night before, Elaine sank into a state of seething indignation, modeling signs of a disgust so pure that Packard felt as if he had returned to the intimate confines of his fifteen-year marriage.

"That coffee almost ready?"

Elaine steps from the van, her streaked hair wild, clamped atop her head inside a device that looks to Packard like something that belongs in a kitchen. An oversized sweatshirt hangs to the middle of her bare thighs, and there's no way of telling what, if anything, she has on underneath—a possibility that provokes in Packard a sudden recollection of her naked bottom flooding his view during their pell-mell escape. Elaine moves close to him, giving off the faint scent of lotion. She runs a hand up his nape and tousles his uncombed hair.

"Quite a night," he says.

Elaine raises the lid of the aluminum coffee pot.

"Not your fault," she agrees.

She starts across the drying grass, heading in flip-flops for the john at the end of the loop. Out in the sunlight, she pivots atop her slender legs and flexed, wrinkled knees.

"And nothing one of those big browns you've been talking about won't cure."

Yet come noon and the menacing heat of the day, not only have temperature gradients generated a wind that bellows down the throat of the canyon, and not only has Elaine failed to hook a fish, big brown or otherwise, but they return to camp for lunch to discover that Packard's ex-wife's tent has vanished.

"Didn't you stake it?" demands Elaine.

"It's got a be around here someplace," counters Packard.

They follow the loop on foot and end up at the host site at the far end of the campground. The wife says that she saw the tent snagged in bushes above the steep drop to the river—but after she went and collected the mail, she forgot all about going back to check on it. Her husband, bridled by plastic tubes to an oxygen tank, states without embellishment that tents like theirs "usually end up in the river." Elaine and Packard hurry back to their campsite and scour the brush, the high bank top and bottom, the edge of the river, both sides of the highway—until they return to camp covered in sweat, dust, and a rash of indelicate scratches, both of them convinced they've learned something invaluable—though they don't know quite what— about the other.

"It's not the end of the world," offers Packard, handing Elaine an open bottle of beer.

"You could say that about most anything," claims Elaine.

After they eat, Elaine dumps her pad and sleeping bag on the grass and collapses in the shade of the fairy tale oak that protects their camp from the worst of the midday sun, one arm draped across her eyes in a posture of exhausted woe. Packard, reheating the last of their morning coffee, fails to come up with a solution to a problem he can't name but feels somehow responsible for. He broods about Elaine's inability to cast the heavy Stone Nymphs favored by the river's big browns, most of them hovering in tight lies amidst the jumbled margins of outsized boulders and shallow, complicated currents. He thinks back to their last day on the Green at the top end of the Seekskadee refuge and the pod of rising cutthroat and a two-foot-long cuttbow hybrid he finally fooled on something small and yellow, a size 20 dun that Elaine did nothing with but drive fish beyond the length of her ragged, frustrated casts. Maybe this is asking too much of her, reasons Packard, a consideration that does nothing to suppress his enthusiasm for returning to the river—once the sun leaves the water—to mix it up with belligerent brown trout that seem more angry than panicked when stung by the hook of a prune-sized nymph.

∾

They're on the road by midafternoon, four or five hours of low light, easing temperatures, a settling wind, and God knows what in the way of burly trout ahead of them. Packard aims the van through the tunnels and enjoys the surge of unfettered optimism that rises in him regardless when and where he goes fishing. Elaine—already, like him, in wading boots, Capilene tights, and wading shorts—directs her gaze toward some inscrutable middle-distance beyond the bug-smeared windshield, her expression giving away nothing that Packard can hang his hopes on.

The highway hugs the course of the river, sometimes approaching its level, usually fifty or even a hundred feet directly above the near bank as the unstable canyon walls converge, towering above the pavement while threatening to shed yet another incomprehensible load of the earth's crust into the blue waters below. Packard drives slowly, considering each turnout across the highway's second lane. Torn between the gnarliest pocket water—where the big browns hold—and the occasional yet less productive riffles and runs, he tries to locate that illogical combination that will somehow satisfy both of them at the same time.

"You have a place picked out?"

Elaine shifts in her seat while at the same time tugging at the visor already pulled low over her eyes.

"Not really."

Packard slows down even more, allowing his focus to swing side to side.

"I'm still just kind of feeling my way around."

Elaine looks at him. She fiddles with the plastic kitchen device crimped to the tangle of hair piled above the visor.

"Just so you know, I didn't like that water we fished this morning."

Elaine tips back her head just enough that for a moment Packard can see her eyes. When she looks away, she keeps her chin tilted upward, the loose skin at her throat held taut.

"I was scared most of the time."

"I had my eye on you," says Packard.

Elaine smiles and then shakes her head.

"Yeah, but it made me nervous. I couldn't help thinking about falling in. It was just too . . . too . . ."

While Elaine searches for the right word, the van sweeps around a curve—and suddenly they approach someone on foot, a guy as gray as Packard coming toward them dragging a cross draped over his shoulder. *A cross,* thinks Packard. *A full-on, crucify-the-Lord-sized cross*—yet on second look he sees that the base of the post, extending a bed's length behind the man, isn't dragging on the pavement at all, but, instead, riding on a tiny wheel.

The fellow—dressed in jeans, sneakers, and a sleeveless T-shirt, his bare arms sunbaked the color of beer bottles—smiles at them and waves as they pass.

"The hell?" says Elaine, twisting in her seat. She tracks the man—and his cross—until the van leaves him around a bend.

"Your last husband?" ventures Packard.

He pulls off at the next turnout. Maybe it's a sign. But Elaine won't hear a word of it. She refuses to go back, a notion Packard advances only because he's suddenly ready to fish. Here? There? He believes it doesn't really matter, that now's the hour and what they

14

need to do is get out and get on the water, putting their flies in the only place they can do any good. Signs or no signs, he thinks, those big brown trout are going to feed, and the only spot they stand to catch one is wherever he and Elaine cast and fish.

Later, Packard will question this reasoning: Wouldn't it all have turned out differently if they had stopped and fished somewhere else?

They leave the van in the turnout and climb down a faint trail that quickly degenerates into a scramble of shifting rock and boulders, the breadth of each growing as they descend nearer the water. Afternoon heat radiates from odd angles off the confusion of jumbled surfaces, until Elaine and Packard lower themselves from the largest boulders and slip down to the very edge of the river itself, where a scrim of cool air stretches across the moving water.

And there's no wind. Packard can't quite figure that, although he's been down at the bottom of plenty enough trout canyons to know that there's not always a rhyme or reason to what does—or doesn't—blow. Maybe, he thinks, Elaine has a chance—a thought he holds onto even after she begins pitching her nymph in arcs of inaccuracy approximating the effects of a catapult rather than any conventional cast common to the sport.

But then she's into a fish. It happens so suddenly that for a moment Packard thinks Elaine is horsing around—a good sign, he tells himself, in the instant between suspecting her nymph of hanging up on the bottom and the immediate, awful bend in her rod, deepening into the cork and accompanied by the shriek of her reel.

Or is it Elaine making that sound? Or—Packard looks about in confusion. Above the roar of the river, outside the audible drama of the woman and the trout, he isolates the sound of squealing tires. Shit. He recalls the precise location of his van, parked on a tangent to the bending highway—and he looks to the top of the bouldery bank and awaits the impact and sound of crunching metal, a sick feeling rising in his bowels.

Yet all he hears is a thud, a loud, deep, resonant thump that could be anything—*could be anything*, thinks Packard, until he sees a deer, a multipoint buck, appear upside down high above the guardrail. The deer cartwheels through the air, headed, it seems, for the river itself—or the two of them—before it loses momentum and collapses halfway down the bank, coming to rest atop a tuft of scrubby brush, where the buck's twisted legs and broken neck duplicate the aspects of snagged, windblown litter.

That evening around the campfire, Elaine produces a bottle of B&B. The seal's already broken. Packard wonders if Elaine has been into the stuff earlier, throughout the trip, or if she just happened to bring an open bottle. He doesn't dare ask.

After their second drink, sipped neat from enameled aluminum cups, Elaine wants to talk again about her fish. While Packard hollered up to the driver of the pickup truck and his wife and two kids, she fought the trout all on her own, somehow keeping it out of the main current, finally guiding it into an eddy tucked in behind a flat, mattress-sized rock. At the same time, Packard grew all but dizzy climbing up to inspect the deer, shouting to the family leaning over the guardrail, and trying to keep track of the commotion down on the water.

"How big do you think it was?" asks Elaine.

"Eight-pointer," answers Packard. "I have to guess close to two hundred pounds."

"No, my fish."

Packard looks into Elaine's firelit eyes.

"Size is measured in increments of fear."

Elaine smiles and shakes her head.

"I've heard you say that at least a hundred times."

"Then why do you keep asking?"

Elaine holds out her cup, motioning Packard for a refill. He points at the bottle standing next to her chair.

"By the way," says Elaine, pouring for both of them, "where do we plan on sleeping?"

Packard rolls his free palm skyward.

"The problem, you know, is all you think about is fish and fishing." Elaine presses the bottle between her knees and twists the cap back on. "That and—well, I don't need to say it."

They both know where this is going.

Two weeks after their return home, Elaine gives Packard another sketch, this one taken from a black-and-white shot of a weathered guide in a Simms catalog she must have found at his house.

And that's that.

# *two*

# Wading Home

When she feels her boots break loose, felt soles skidding with the current, Sarah Newell manages a flurry of awkward gestures that seem to her, in their very midst, the stuff of lowest comedy.

For a moment she thinks she might stay put, stop short of a serious drenching. Her movement, downstream, suggests the languid pace of flight in dreams. But as she kicks through the water, scraping her boots against rock, she recognizes she is already moving too quickly; she can't possibly stop herself now. *Swimming*, thinks Sarah Newell, dragging her rod through the current, cold water spilling over the tops of her waders—and at the same moment she names her predicament, the thought of it is replaced with an image of the coyote she watched, that winter, carried through the rapids at Rattlesnake campground, not fifty yards downstream from where the Deschutes now draws her inextricably into its potent embrace.

Yet from the outset it seems almost a release, this floating at the margin of the wide river, the water cool beneath the press of hot dry air fueled by sunlight pouring into the jagged tear of the high desert canyon—release, moreover, from the weight of culpability that everyone in her life of late seems so quick to calculate in response to her every mistake, shortcoming, or failure to please. She feels, instead—what?—content, she decides, or suddenly free, at a loss to do anything more than ride this thing out—just like the coyote, she recalls, its head held high, bobbing through the standing waves of the downstream rapid while she and David, a new distraction in her life, watched from the bank through the sparkling light of an icy white-fish outing two days before Valentine's.

She certainly feels no sense of danger. An ocean swimmer in California since she could barely walk, she has absolutely no fear around water except when faced with the dangerous riptides associated with large surf or threatened by the presence of sharks. Or waterfalls, she thinks, amused by the notion until she remembers for the first time in years that a cousin of hers, a son of her mother's only sister, died three decades earlier at Shear's Falls, fifteen miles upriver, an accident no one in the family offered explanation for beyond the alcohol involved and the categorical foolishness of attempting to survive the falls' murderous hydraulics. Drawn into heavier current, she feels the subtle sensation of acceleration, akin, she notes, to the surge of a lifting wave, although infinitely slower, she decides—and in the deliberate, gradual build-up to the rapids themselves she pictures again the little buff-colored coyote rising and falling through the chain of ragged waves, an act of comic submission, she remembers thinking, the coyote's face and beady eyes expressionless, without trace of concern or even effort as it held itself upright, dog-paddling down the throat of the rapids before settling into the wide eddy and curling off toward the steep rocks worn smooth by eons of current.

"Fucking A," said David, his voice breathy, reverential. And even then, Sarah recalls, gliding with the river, one hand on her favorite two-hander, the other, having already drawn her wading belt tight, now circling just beneath the surface, balancing her while her booted feet and buoyant legs tread water below—even then, she thinks, she might have been warned, before she knew what this tone would come to mean, how she felt she had just been commanded to respond in a certain way, while her wannabe lover squeezed her hand as though the scene before them were somehow his doing.

At the lip of the chute, Sarah's downstream progress abruptly stops. She's spun by the current, lifted and pulled straight and forced flat on her stomach into the surging surface before she understands that her rod or line has snagged on something. Head up, current pressed to her neck, she tightens her grip; she refuses to let go of the most expensive piece of sporting equipment she's ever owned. The rod flexes and bucks and she's surprised nothing breaks, and then she can feel the rod vibrating in her hand, a kind of profound tuning-fork vibration that she suddenly connects to the pale gray branch poking, just upstream, through the current, holding her in place as if a stake linked to a dog's chain.

For a moment she thinks she's strong enough to pull herself up the rod, climb all thirteen feet of it hand over hand and manage somehow to untangle it or break the branch or even the tip of the rod itself so that she doesn't lose everything. Then she knows it's impossible. Glare off the water distorts her vision, playing a queer trick on perspective so that the exposed tip of the offending snag appears suddenly a distant buoy across a vast reach of ocean. She swipes at her eyes and realizes her sunglasses are gone, croakie and all, plus her hat—and it's her sudden recognition that these things vanished, and she doesn't know when and how, that brings her fully aware of her situation, the overpowering strength of the river, and the first trace of fear that has penetrated her effortless cool.

Still, she remains fast to the rod. *Forty-two fucking years old,* she thinks fiercely, *fit as a fucking twenty-year-old, strong enough to hang*

21

*on tight in the fucking Deschutes river—and I'm worried about—what?*
*Losing my pretty blue Thomas & Thomas rod? Having to cry for help?*
*Needing another fucking man to bail me out?*

Questions and self-pity aside, Sarah Newell holds on until the
water forced by the heavy current past her wading belt swells the legs
of her waders to a point of resistance that overwhelms her formi-
dable strength and determination. Letting go the rod, she tips immediately upright, buoyed by the zero-gravity sensation of her body
encased in water—and once again she pictures the coyote she spied
dog-paddling downstream, by choice or accident she'd wondered
ever since—and now she mimics the animal's abject posture and loss
of control, bobbing effortlessly and without incident through the
rapids' standing waves, with little the chance observer would have
seen to distinguish her from the coyote itself but the sudden tears in
her eyes.

A half-hour later, Sarah feels it was all somehow a silly scare. Naked
save for a prudent black sports thong purchased from Patagonia
but never yet shown anyone else—not even her husband Rail—she
warms herself amidst the drying clothes spread atop the same rock
shelf onto which she and David had watched the coyote climb before
shaking itself dry, the water, leaping from its coat, radiant in the winter sunlight, yet capable of freezing, she remembers thinking, before
showering the ice beneath its paws. Seated, propped up on her arms
behind her, she imagines herself an old lizard basking in the over-
head sun, a picture she immediately rejects as she studies the sun-
damaged skin running past her knees before finally fading into the
pale recesses of her outstretched thighs. She closes her eyes deliber-
ately. She studies the patterns of the harsh light's afterimages swirling inside her eyelids, a sensation her brother had claimed since they
were grade-schoolers was the closest thing anyone got to reliving the
past. Were he here to see her now, she thinks, her eyes still closed,

relishing the warmth of the smooth rock beneath her, painful at first to touch though she was shivering convulsively by the time she had removed her boots and bloated waders and briefly debated whether she should remove her drenched undergarments at all.

The thought of her brother Phil, dead now only three months, produces in Sarah a slow contraction at the base of her sternum, a steady tightening that expands through her ribcage and leaves her all but breathless. What would he have said, she wonders, had he found her sitting here like this now? The consummate big brother, no doubt he would have told her to cover up, "stop casting bait" or some such awful innuendo—the very same sort of remark he made on a family Baja trip the first time she needed tampons and he caught her removing one in the ill-defined "kybow" area, the latrine, in the sand dunes beyond camp. Phil's death, fears Sarah, has made the rest of the men in her life superfluous. She suddenly grows self-conscious about her bare legs and naked breasts, and as she pulls the damp Capilene top over her head she wishes desperately she could carry on some sort of conversation with the dead, a trick she has attempted repeatedly the past three months while feeling certain she has read far too many stories in which characters enjoy this good fortune for the possibility of it to be real.

Still, she has little trouble imagining her brother, dead or alive, advising her to get dressed and get back across the river—unless she wants the latest rendition of Prince Charming to come to her soggy-ass rescue. And all that implies. She feels the sweat already rising against the fabric tight to her skin, and she recalls her brother teasing her day after day at the end of workouts before her first lifeguard tryouts because she was a girl and she couldn't "go down to skin." Furious the day after she was selected an alternate rather than a full-time summer guard, she kept as close to her brother as she could during their final hundred yard sprint through the deep sand approaching the pier, and as they strolled about catching their breath in the shadows between the pilings, she suddenly pulled off her T-shirt and new sports bra and stood in front of her brother as if she didn't care who saw her young pale breasts. Whether he was surprised or not, she couldn't tell, as he glanced at her for but a moment before he turned away and took off running again down the beach while she hurriedly pulled on her clothes.

An hour passes and Sarah is still standing waist-deep in the river, having decided she has no reason to hurry back to the other side in the steamy confines of her wading garments. The occasional truck or SUV kicks up dust in the distance, while on the water three rafts and a drift boat have slid by within casting distance, not one person spotting her after she caught sight of each group far upstream and then held perfectly still, verifying her conviction that unless something moves, people only see what they expect to see. She recalls the look of incomprehension that clung to Rail's face when he found her masturbating—or beginning to—while soaking in their backyard hot tub after the cold day on the river with David when they watched the coyote cross and, later, in his truck, they made out like teenagers in the empty campground at Jones Canyon. She wonders what more Rail suspects about her relationship with David, her speculation free of guilt by force of her decision—at whatever cost to David—to restrict any hanky-panky to well-spaced sessions of necking and heavy petting.

But this show of faithfulness, she thinks, the chill of the water swimming around her thighs, serves only to heighten her sense of inadequacy, as she sees herself unwilling to leave a pointless marriage yet thoroughly convinced she needs a lover like she needs a kick in the teeth. "Fuck them," she says out loud, a feeling about men she traces directly back to her brother's sudden departure from her life, his long descent into isolation, and whatever carried him to his end. She looks upstream as far as she can see, scans the long sweep of cottonwoods tilted as if ready to fall into the river, the road atop the old railroad grade beyond them, the somber face of the shaded canyon wall. Except for the water, nothing seems to move. She wonders, if she waits long enough, who will show up first, David or Rail.

"Fuck them both," she thinks bitterly, unwilling to let herself start crying again after the wave of grief she rode through the rapids. She lifts the hem of her top and settles again into the river, the water rising past the silly thong and up over her firm belly, the sun, lower now, sharp against her nose and cheeks. She lets the bottom of the shirt fall and runs her hands through the water and lifts it to her face. She draws in a slow breath that seems to expand her submerged pelvis and she wishes simply for her brother's lasting peace, a thought she is sure means nothing but is the very best she or anyone can do.

Dry once more and wadered, the sun slipping toward the lip of the canyon, Sarah rummages through her vest and a little emergency dry bag, stashed in the pouch of her waders before leaving her Subaru in a turnout upriver between Cedar Island and the top of the long run of broken, complex water that has both delighted and bruised her and her ego for as long as she's searched for steelhead willing to rise to the fly. She expects to find nothing but her usual meager snack—today a packet of trail mix and a single, flattened granola bar. Eating, she pictures the avocado and Swiss cheese on rye sandwich she impulsively laced that morning with a slice of raw onion and a shower of ground pepper before squeezing it into a baggie and setting it neatly atop two Fuji apples, a baggie full of tortilla chips, and three homemade oatmeal cookies inside the one-person ice chest now on the floor in front of the passenger-side seat. And the thermos of coffee and her cell phone—the latter useless in the canyon. She finishes off her ration of store-bought water and returns the plastic bottle down the zippered slit at the back of her vest. Curious, she digs two fingers down to the bottom of the little dry bag, finding matches,

25

two Band-Aids, a tampon, a tube of Blistex, ibuprofen—until she's reminded of her brother demanding during her sophomore year in high school that she always carry a twenty-dollar bill and a condom in her purse because if something happened, he said, it didn't matter whose fault it was, a woman was the one who had to live with the consequences of her actions.

The sun dips from view. Sunlight recedes from a small portion of the river, but at a pace so slow that she quickly loses interest in watching the progress—or regress—she can't decide what it is she's actually looking at. Or *for*, she concludes, glancing up and down the road for a vehicle coming in either direction. In the shade she feels the cool of the river rise up and erase the heat, as if someone had opened the windows of a house, and she recalls waiting summer evenings near Tamarack along Pacific Coast Highway for one of her parents to pick her up long after her shifts ended. She never knew when they would arrive. Research professors at UCSD, they had both drifted so far apart and so deeply into their separate laboratories that they remained available to her for only the most rudimentary attention. Other guards and surfers stopped and offered her rides, but her brother had told her that if she rode home with anyone he'd hear about it and "kick the shit out of" whoever it was, a threat she believed with the certainty of sunrise even though it had been delivered as matter-of-factly as a promise to help with her algebra homework.

She stands at the edge of the water as if waiting for something and then realizes that her unsettled state of mind is due in part to the fact that she's poised here along this blessed river in ebbing light without her fishing rod. There could be steelhead holding at the edge of the big eddy directly in front of her, their mere existence a possibility she finds too staggering to consider beyond the simple notion of fish swimming in a river. She feels sick again about losing her rod, not because she cares anything about catching a steelhead right now, she tells herself, but because it was hers, paid for with her own money, the very first rod she ever shopped for and selected all by herself, and she still savors the irrational view that no two fly rods cast exactly alike.

But "gone is gone," as her brother used to say. And for the first time since getting swept down the river she pictures him in a harsher relief, no longer merely a big brother anymore but closer to yet another man in her life, remote, elusive, enigmatic—or was he simply, by then, withdrawn? He appeared unannounced at her wedding, five years after she had last seen him at their mother's funeral, which mercifully followed less than two months after the death of their father, a victim, implausibly, of heart failure at the age of sixty-five. Whether her mother had a hand in her own death, as her mother's sister suggested, seemed to Sarah so far removed from anyone else's business that she simply shelved the issue alongside questions of an afterlife. At the wedding and reception her brother seemed smaller than he used to be, but in truth how would she know, he remained for her larger than life, moving about the festivities in a tailored sports jacket and new Levi's, a black shirt with mother-of-pearl buttons, a pair of topsiders that appeared dark as black coffee with oiling. And no socks. The lack of socks infuriated her. How could she take him seriously? How *couldn't* she? Except for this complete disregard for appearances, he looked as if he had never been surfing in all his life. No socks in winter in Bend. She didn't know the last time he had seen the ocean. Or even which one. She wanted to impress Rail and all of his snowboard buddies, give them a glimpse of her own sporting bloodlines beyond her manic efforts to keep up with them, to prove herself worthy of their—what? Company? Respect? Locker room jokes? Gallons of weekend beer? But Phil wouldn't—or couldn't—engage. What was wrong with him? *Was* there anything wrong? Even back then?

27

"He looks like some sort of gnostic waif," wrote David after she emailed him Phil's picture, the last one she saw of her brother, six months before he was found dead in an overturned Jaguar a hundred yards off Highway 6 somewhere between Ely and Tonopah in the Nevada desert. "He looks like he's been looking for God so hard he forgot to pay his water bill."

She laughed reading that. This was exactly what she liked about David, his humor, the rich language, the odd things he said that made perfect sense to her. Ten years with Rail and he still just wanted to get air. Get happy. Get hammered. Get laid. She had no one to blame but herself. And now—of course—David is just as eager as the next guy to get her undressed—"Get on with it," he has begun to say.

She had no idea where the picture came from, where it was taken, how Phil had even known where to send it. But the latter was no issue whatsoever. It's the twenty-first century, for Christ's sake, she thinks; even a Luddite like Phil could find her online. The picture was in an email titled "Yours." There were no other words, just her brother, fur-chested, red board shorts riding low on his still-slender hips, the incongruous gray whiskers, the haircut of a Buddhist monk, the wiry frame, his pale, pale eyes—all of it some sort of testimony but she couldn't tell to what because every time she looked again at the picture, or saw it in her mind's eye, her attention was drawn unremittingly to the line of surf in the background, which she knew was her clue to where Phil had been, and to the hand of an arm wrapped around her brother's waist, the hand of someone otherwise hidden or cropped from the frame.

"Nothing was wrong with him," said the state patrolman assigned to call the next of kin. "No alcohol. No drugs. Must've fallen asleep."

"In the middle of the day?" she asked, already trying to make sense of a world in which her brother no longer existed.

"People get tired at any hour, ma'am. 'Specially when they're alone."

But he *hadn't* been alone, she felt like shouting into the phone. Not six months ago, not ever. He knew without question, she believed, how deeply she cared for him, how she admired him, idolized him. He had no right to even *feel* alone, she argued insensibly with herself, an argument she soon knew she would never win, just as she knew—if she knew anything about their lives—that her brother had sent that picture because of the hidden person in it, so that she, his sister, would never know who it was, what she, the girl, the woman looked like—nor how she, whoever it was, looked at him.

It's Rail who shows up first.

She sees his 4Runner coming up the road from Macks Canyon, his Spey rod extending from the rack on the hood up over the cab like an oversized antenna. He slows down above the Rattlesnake campground—certainly looking for her—and then he speeds off upriver and out of view. Minutes later, the Toyota comes creeping back down the road, Rail having spotted her car, no doubt, and now searching through the trees for sign of her at water's edge.

The arrangement for the day had been simple enough; more and more they both agreed they needed to take every opportunity possible to stay out of each other's way. It made perfect sense steelheading. Cover more runs, said Rail, you cover more water. Early in the season, their chances of finding a fish were slim enough. They certainly weren't going to risk the kind of blowups they were prone to of late by spending a day together in Rail's boat. They had driven up from Bend before first light, taking separate vehicles for a number of hollow pretenses: While Rail headed down to Macks to claim a camp site, she could start fishing; if Rail wanted to spend the night and fish the following morning, he was free to stay; they both had favorite runs they could give their full attention to; cover more runs, you cover more water.

Rail's rig disappears behind the wall of willows on the far bank as he leaves the road and drops into the campground. Sarah thinks she can hear the engine shut down but she isn't sure. She waits for the sound of a door closing, only to be startled by a pair of mergansers, their wings beating like the legs of sprinters, that veer off sharply to avoid passing directly over her head. Sunlight has left the canyon, and the sound of the ducks, rushing upstream, seems to hang above the river as if footfall in an empty room. She follows the birds until they vanish around the bend, expecting any moment to see another boat float into view. If she's going to get wet, she decides, she had better do it soon.

When David's pickup appears, stirring dust not yet settled from both passes by Rail, she feels more despondent than fearful of the inevitable consequences of her duplicity. David's speed, she notes, replicates Rail's exactly. Near the top of each thigh she feels a light vibration, much like the feel of the branch, shuddering in the current, on which she lost her rod. Her knees and ankles ache, and she realizes she has been standing still for so long, at the edge of the water, that she can't place the surface of her skin inside the baggy weight of her waders.

David slows and turns into the campground. She had told him she'd be fishing along the lower access road. He said he'd probably hang out around Beavertail; maybe he'd run into her. She wades in up to her knees. Men never *just run into you*, she thinks. They come looking for you like heat-seeking missiles.

She studies the break in the willows, the water up to her waist. A breath of wind runs across the surface of the eddy, the temperature gradients sorting themselves out. Bowed limbs sway about the gap of the path. She hears voices. Both men know each other, know about each other, in the way, she thinks, they must always know in situations like these. The trick is never to lie, she thinks, but keep the truth sealed in your heart.

She checks her wading belt and edges into the river, her eyes drawn to the confused currents twisting below the last tumble of rapids before unraveling and sliding off in a gentle sweep of gathering energy. She remembers standing in a similar light near day's end, half her broken board under one arm following a vicious wipeout and exhausting swim on a huge day at Petacalco along the jungled coast of Michoacan. She relished the feel of the coarse gritty sand stirred by the shorebreak, the solid ground beneath her feet. Outside, her brother took off late on a set wave that stopped her breathing until he made the drop and pulled off one of his signature turns and set up for a barrel that stopped her breathing again. There was nothing to do but wait—and when her brother reappeared, seemingly alone in the cosmos, she knew that if she continued to try to keep up with him, she would die trying.

The water nears the tops of her waders before she feels herself lifting off her feet. Rail and David stand beneath the willows, looking upstream and down. Through the fading light she makes out their expressions of concern, whether for her or their own uncertain futures, she can't tell which.

Let them figure it out, she thinks, pushing free of the bottom. Dog-paddling, she starts back across the river, wondering where she'll end up downstream.

# *three*

# Twenty Minutes More

The shop is near the river by the tavern where he used to meet an old construction buddy for beer and fries while taking a break from studies for his master's. The place advertises itself as a canoe dealer but turns out to push kayaks. They can get them what they want, the sales guy says, but they'll have to share the shipping costs split two ways. His wife wants to close the deal.

"We don't even know what color we want," he protests. His wife and the sales guy look at him as if that just might be a decision they are going to have to make. He refuses, motioning toward the door.

"I thought we agreed we definitely weren't going to buy today," he argues as soon as they step outside.

"He said he can get us whatever we want. What are we *waiting* for?"

"Sand or Eggplant?" he counters. "Green or Cherry?" His wife closes her eyes. She takes a slow, deep breath. "There's no way you and I can decide these things right now," he adds.

33

"I hate Eggplant."

"What about wood gunwales? Or do you get vinyl? Or aluminum?"

"I'd never want aluminum."

"Do you like the St. Croix paddle or the Koyuluk?"

"Okay! Okay!" His wife places a hand flat beneath her throat. Her breath is shallow, her fingers fluttering like pages of a book left out in the wind. "Then how about if we just go over to REI and see what a rack for the van would cost?"

The color Sand turns out to be almost identical to that of the manila folders in which he keeps his newly composed lesson plans. Highlighted by ash gunwales, the color contrasts handsomely with the forest-green carpet of the showroom floor. His wife hands the REI clerk her Platinum Fleet card. Beside her, he quietly admires the sophisticated engineering of the interchangeable components of their new Yakima rack system. Lifting the canoe front and back, two clerks ask where they are parked.

The slough channel leads into a broad, shallow lake surrounded on all sides by oaks and willows and tall cottonwoods, forested mountains in the distance, a bucolic scene of deep greens and solitude. Stillwater reflects the cloudless sky. A blue heron rises from the shore. Here and there, large fish roll on the surface, marring the glassy texture and making his heart ache.

The dog's sudden barking reminds him of the nature of the outing. He spots a paddler dressed like a Tour de France cyclist emerge inside a yellow sliver of plastic from a break in the trees. The gentle flex of his own laminated hardwood paddle steers them through a sharp turn as he avoids this, the only other person on the water, as if the kayaker is pushing a shopping cart down a dark alley. His wife glances back at him, her own paddle raised, as if to consider what she might have done wrong to cause this abrupt change of course. He gestures at the kayaker and then the dog, silently praying they won't have to put up with another twenty minutes of panicked barking while she, the dog, settles down once more.

Fish keep rolling. By the time they retreat up the slough channel to where they parked the van, he is sure the fish are carp, a hasty identification made upon lifting a carcass found floating just beneath the surface, only to set the dog off again. Out of respect for this sort of family outing—their son this morning has even brought along a friend—he is without a rod in the canoe, an absolutely unacceptable practice he intends to rectify as soon as he can screw up the courage to broach the subject with his wife. These rolling carp, however, have gone a long way in laying the groundwork for his case, as his wife knows as well as he does that even a dog shouldn't be expected to act like anything but a dog, metaphorically speaking.

Back at the launch site, he dives into a recent history of the growing popularity of carp in the sport of fly fishing, how even John Gierach writes about carp, and even Seth Norman once had his picture with a carp on the cover of a magazine.

"What about Tom Hughes?" his wife asks.

"Dave," he says. "His name is *Dave* Hughes."

"Well, what about him? Does he like carp?"

"I don't know. I never asked him."

"Do you even know Tom Hughes?"

"Dave," he says. "His name is Dave."

They finish lunch and get the canoe strapped on and the boys and dog settled into the van. A Nissan beater pulls into the gravel lot. The rusted door swings open and an old-timer dressed in jeans and a dirty T-shirt and canvas sneakers climbs out carrying a crumpled plastic milk jug. He nods as he walks past them and then starts down the steep bank toward the water. Nearly there he slips and falls, skidding down the mud, going in all the way up to his waist. He can't get out.

"You need a hand?"

He doesn't wait for the old guy to answer, grabbing a paddle from the back of the van.

"I could use one!"

Later, he and his wife will argue over how long the old guy might have been stuck had they not been there to help. The channel drops off abruptly, the clay slick as oil, so that it is nearly impossible to climb up the bank without holding onto something. He gets the old guy to move over to where he can brace his Aquasocks against a knot of roots. Finally he's able to reach the blade of the paddle to him, pull him out on his hands and knees—not a lifesaving rescue, but the old guy is huffing and puffing pretty seriously by the time they are both up on flat ground.

"I just . . . . needed some water . . . . for that damn radiator."

The car makes clicking noises in the midday sun. They fill the bottle from a jug in the back of the van. Swimming has worn out the dog enough that she ignores the presence of a stranger in the same parking lot. The boys sit giggling inside until his wife shushes them. The old guy sets the water on the backseat of his car and then sits in the front with his feet out as if trying to decide whether or not he wants to muddy the inside.

"Nice canoe you got there," he says, bending forward, his breathing still heavy. He reaches out and begins to unlace his sneakers. "You been carp fishing?"

He looks over at his wife. She is already looking at him. "Not yet," he says. "Just looking around."

"Glad you were." The old-timer pushes off the back of one shoe with the toe of the other. "Had to be some other good reason you were here than to pull my dirty hide outa the drink."

The rule is simple: He has twenty minutes, total, to fish, taken in chunks or all at once, beginning with the time of the first cast, clock stops whenever he says he's not actually fishing.

He knows it's absurd. Twenty minutes. A man of his . . . stature. But there you have it. He descends the stairs to his basement office, wondering which rod to choose.

At least it's a start. Most of their outings remain exercises in loading and unloading the canoe, finding and launching in new water, trying to make a routine out of it all, fit it into their lives. Not that he has begun camping out on the couch, he reminds himself, imagining his son's iPod in one hand, the new Pottery Barn catalogue in the other. He decides to go with the five-weight.

They put in at the boat ramp on Scappoose Bay. Gray clouds hang just above the tree tops. Waves of gentle rain ride an indecisive breeze out of the south. He is still having trouble figuring the difference between times given for the nearest tide station, and he is surprised when they reach the middle of the bay and he can touch bottom with his paddle. They cross over to the far side and swing around an island into a channel he thinks might be one of the creeks he has seen entering the bay on the map. In the still, slick, nearly brown water at the mouth of the channel, he sees a fish roll. He announces he is putting up his rod.

"You're going to start fishing?" asks their son, seated alongside the yoke, aware of the recent negotiations regarding allotted time. The boy has been on banks across the state, waiting hour after hour, too.

"No, I'm just getting ready." He unscrews the end of the rod tube. "Your mother can check her watch when I make my first cast."

He strings up and, with an unusual lack of hesitation, ties on what he is calling his dragonfly nymph, an Art Scheck take-off on Polly Rosbourough's Casual Dress nymph tied completely out of bunny fur clipped from Zonker strips. Aaeschnid and gomphid specimens

37

collected throughout the spring are still terrorizing the smaller, more benign macroinvertebrates in his classroom aquariums, and he has concluded that short of tadpoles and forage fish, your big dragonfly nymph is as good as any meal to move a predaceous carnivore in the stillwaters of an estuarial floodplain. Speculation, he thinks, but where else to begin?

The critical moment comes the first time the big nymph and double-tapered line roar past his wife's head. She hasn't quite counted on that. He lets the fly sink, soaking the fur, then picks up and lets fly again, sensing his wife's neck shorten, her chin inch down her chest.

"Did you check your watch?" he says.

She has. Near the five minute mark he gets a couple of tugs and hooks and lands a tiny largemouth bass. He asks his wife, in the bow, to put her paddle in the water on the left side of the canoe and take one soft stroke backwards. She does, without comment, the canoe moving smartly back into position.

"Thank you," he says.

After a few more casts he reels up and hooks the dripping nymph in the keeper.

"You done fishing?" asks their son.

"For now," he says, placing the rod out of the way. "How much time left?"

"Thirteen minutes." His wife looks directly at him. "You know, I can do this if I know it's not going to last indefinitely."

They paddle up the creek until it dead-ends in a tangle of driftwood. A blue heron leads them back toward the main channel, stopping just beyond each bend until they again glide into view. A pair of teal and a raft of fledglings cross the creek and disappear under the bare trunk of a fallen cottonwood settling into the mud. He sees a fish roll here, another there, and each time he makes a few casts as his wife holds the canoe in position and keeps track of time.

38

Back near where he caught the one tiny bass, he realizes they are about finished. He resigns himself to one last flurry of casts. Another fish rolls, bending reflections in the quiet water, and he replicates yet another cast into the fold.

"Let me ask you this," he says, watching his line as he strips in the fly. "Suppose there's a minute or two left and I hook a big fish and while I'm fighting it my twenty minutes run out. Do I have to break off the fish?"

He throws his backcast, shoots for the spot he has hit three times in a row. His wife turns and faces their son.

"What do you think?" she asks.

"I think it's up to you," says the boy.

After several more casts, his wife speaks up again.

"You know, there's a fish or something I keep seeing over there." She motions with her paddle toward the open water of the bay. "I think that's your chance, not here."

"How much time's left?"

"A couple minutes."

They paddle out of the channel, just beyond the small island at the edge of the bay. He makes a cast and lets the fly sink. He watches his line straighten, and it begins to move.

"My God, he took it! He's on!"

The fish is good, peeling line off the reel.

"Can you *believe* it?" his wife says to their son.

With the five-weight he doesn't have much control over the fish, and it swims in all directions, first one way and then the other, searching for a way free. He just hangs on, laughing and talking, gaining a little line here and there, losing a little less each time the fish panics. They are all pretty giddy.

"Can you believe it?" repeats his wife. "Your dad hooked the fish in the very last minute."

39

He gets the fish up to the boat and they admire its brilliant colors, the bronze and greens and golds more like an agate than an animal. It is all but finished, its large mouth opening and closing as if gasping for air. He grabs ahold of the big nymph and twists it free. The fish hangs just beneath the surface of the dark water then fades away.

"Carp," he says. "I just knew that's what we were seeing."

"That was a nice fish," says his wife. She turns to their son. "I guess twenty minutes is just about perfect."

*four*

# Slate
# Blue

He knows he's in trouble when she comes out from behind the Subaru, still in her sun dress, her bare legs tapering dramatically into a pair of heavy-soled leather brogues. The dress, an unripe apple green, seemed innocent enough as they drove across the state in the dense July heat, tracing the margins of a vast smear of smoky sky fed by wildfires in the distant mountains. The straps at her sharp collarbones left her toned arms free to steer, and only once, behind his sunglasses, had he suffered several miles of foolish thoughts, lost in study of the delicate veining along the inside of her far bicep. The hem, to be sure, had ridden, on occasion, high on her thighs as she stirred beneath the wheel, forcing him to avert his eyes. But at Elgin Fischer's age, *all* dresses seem short, if only because so few women wear them anymore—although there also remains, for him, the simple consideration of their remarkable, panoramic access.

It's the shoes, however, laced beneath Eudora Cromwell's slender ankles and trim, athletic calves, that threaten to do Elgin in. His heart, he feels, possesses no means to resist such flagrant disregard for pretense or décor. He peers over the tops of his reading glasses, set in place so that he can rebuild Dori's leader, a collection of wind knots and brittle blood knots from whenever she last went fishing. He fumbles with the spools of tippet material he found stashed in her fanny pack, probably the same spools, he thinks, from the last time they fished together. Hell, this could be the same damn leader, he concludes, not quite certain how many years ago he invited her to meet him for that August evening on the Deschutes.

"You got flies?" he asks, reaching again for the clippers he expects—third time and counting—to find dangling from his vest. Annoyed, he thrusts a hand down a front pocket of his shorts, finding his keys, the clippers there. No vest; no tippet; no flies. No rod or reel or waders, he chides himself, incapable of appreciating the irony of his negligence as Dori Cromwell rests a shoe on the bumper of her Subaru and lathers her leg with sunscreen above the hard bones of her cocked knee.

"There's a box there with something in it," she says, gesturing with her head toward the fanny pack as she shifts her ministrations, spreading sunscreen as if washing her hands and arms.

Elgin locates the fly box, relieved to find beneath the clear plastic lid a neat row of Adamses and a half-dozen brand-new Yellow Humpys, shiny as gems, probably a size too big but he doubts it'll matter, if there are fish in the river they can at least get one to rise. Maybe this will work after all, he thinks, still astounded or maybe troubled—he isn't sure what he feels—that he showed up without fishing gear while Dori brought hers. "Of course I did," she announced when he loaded his duffel bag and daypack into the Subaru and commented on the rod tube there. "I figured you have yours with you wherever you go."

Was she disappointed? He knots a Humpy to the tippet, glancing over the tops of his glasses while Dori finishes shielding herself from the harsh midafternoon sun. In Elgin Fischer's long and varied history of relationships with women, he has suffered most whenever he felt he has let them down, to the point that, in the end, all of his relationships with women seem draped in a dark veil of his own mistakes, his inadequacies and failures, a sheer black fabric behind which women mourn his inability to make them permanently happy. He has been single, more or less, for five years now, not the happiest period of his life but certainly the smoothest, a long stretch of solitude, reflection, gentle despair—and more damn fish than he could have possibly ever imagined.

Somewhere between Pendleton and La Grande he has managed to quiet most of his misgivings and settled into the prospects of serving as Dori Cromwell's guide, offering the kind of attention he recognizes as next to impossible should he have a rod of his own in hand. This will be fun, he decided, the Subaru cresting a pass in the Blue Mountains, leaving behind the haze and descending into the upper reaches of the Grande Ronde. No pressure. No expectations. They'll get in the water and he'll help her see what she can find.

But he hasn't anticipated the shoes, the summer dress as wading attire, her readiness to step into the river with him at her side. Elgin hands her the rod and finds his sneakers at the bottom of his daypack, brought along because he knew they would probably want to run, part of his own routine, as well, any day he doesn't fish. Clearly Dori's been running, too, notes Elgin, or getting exercise of some sort, her body taut as a twenty-year-old's between the loose skin and creases and sun-damaged surfaces of a woman at least as old as any of his three sisters. He knots the laces of his shoes, inspecting the blemished, nearly hairless skin of his pale, aged ankles. This'll be fun, he tells himself again, although he can't quite shake the feeling that, for the second time in his life, he is already falling in love with Dori Cromwell.

43

∽

A decade earlier, it hadn't made any sense—nor amounted to much—either.

She came from wealth, family, a name everyone recognized even if most of them would be pressed to identify a context. At the start, he certainly didn't know the difference between a Cromwell and King Tut, although by that point in his life, Elgin Fischer had begun to distance himself from the world around him, slipping into an all but private universe inhabited by steelhead, trout, and the rivers where he encountered these coldwater species with fly rods and flies. This same period proved especially unsettling for Elgin's family and friends, who found it increasingly difficult to penetrate his sharply delineated passions, leaving those around him feeling removed from this private source of gravity around which Elgin seemed to orbit. By the time he met Dori Cromwell, Elgin wasn't so much alone in the world as he was unaware that anything he did anymore mattered to anyone but him.

His counselor at the time suggested that he try writing—*journaling* she called it, a way for Elgin to *concretize* (again, the counselor's word) his thoughts so that he might better articulate ideas and communicate them to his wife and two teenage daughters. Carol wasn't really Elgin's counselor, but a family and marriage advisor Elgin's wife had met at the New Thought Christian Church she demanded the family attend. Elgin found Carol pleasant enough, a tall, broad-shouldered woman somewhere between the age of his wife and daughters, with pretty blonde hair and inviting hips that he studied while listening to his wife explain her disappointment in his behavior. Eventually Elgin began meeting alone with Carol, his wife having decided that the woman couldn't be trusted, that she was taken in by Elgin's quiet demeanor and willingness to listen and, worst of all, she failed to see the subtleties of his contemptible behavior.

Elgin purchased a hand-stitched rufous-colored leather journal, the size of a paperback novel, with a clever set of interlocking loops, much like the matching pivot-points of a hinge, where he could keep a ballpoint pen. He found the journaling idea silly; he often communicated to his wife and daughters exactly what he thought about fish and fishing, rivers and streams, flies and fly rods and fly lines and casts he could and sometimes still couldn't make. But his family had heard most of his thoughts and observations before, and now they didn't really care to hear more. What most disappointed his wife, Elgin understood, was not that he had allowed his world to shrink to the margins of the sport of fly fishing, but that he remained hopeful he could show her some small thing in that world she would care about, a possibility she could no longer entertain.

Still, Elgin felt compelled to write. A teacher, he honored the notion of assignments, doing them no matter how little one understood their purpose or practicality. There was, as well, for Elgin a sense of getting his money's worth—not that he actually paid for Carol's services, but somebody did, his medical insurance, the system if you will—and in Elgin's view of the world there needed to exist a balanced economy of input and output, goods received for the energy required to obtain them, just as a trout needed to gain more or at least as much in the way of energy and nutrition for the effort it took to feed. To ignore the counselor's suggestion to write would have seemed to Elgin inefficient, perhaps even profligate—and there was also for him his exaggerated concern with disappointing even Carol, she of the inviting hips, his opinion of which he kept to himself although he suspected she knew full well.

His sense of economy and equivalencies, of balance and approbation, even Elgin's painful concern with disappointing women conspired with his writing assignments into the composition of poetry. He pieced together a few images and ideas, words he liked, thoughts he had. He wondered if these were really poems. His high school's

shop teacher, he began to wander the halls of the English department, thumbing through textbooks and asking teachers there—
mostly women, three of them young mothers—what poems they
taught, which ones they especially liked. Elgin listened not so much
for the names of poems and poets but for the tone in the teachers'
voices, the excitement they brought to the poems, the emotional
response the poems inspired, which somehow seemed to him associated with a passion that had nothing to do, as far as he could tell, with
good poetry and bad poetry, but instead seemed a response as simple
and mysterious as a steelhead's response to one cast or fly and not a
dozen others. He enjoyed listening to the teachers talk about poems
in much the same way that, at this point in his life, he could stop fishing during the middle of a hatch and watch trout feed, watch them
"cavort like leprechauns" as he described in one poem, although he
wasn't sure that was exactly right, having never seen a leprechaun,
and didn't cavorting, Elgin asked himself, imply pleasure, or frivolity,
which, thinking of feeding trout, seemed a stretch of the imagination. The teachers—especially the women—proved determined to
make certain he understood what they loved about the poems they
described, and Elgin would sit quietly and listen to their animated
talk, not particularly interested in what they had to say, but instead
studying their eyes and mouths and especially the changing colors
of the flesh about their cheeks and necks, the flush of blood at their
throats or the tips of their ears were they exposed. All of this Elgin
took in as he would the behavior of an individual feeding trout, the
mood of the trout as revealed to him by signals so subtle he felt certain, at times, they were both real and imagined, a projection of what
he believed about a trout he wanted to catch—although he still felt it
next to impossible to stand and watch a feeding fish for long without
attempting to fool it with a fly.

When Elgin heard about a summer writing conference in the
northeast corner of the state, a region he had somehow failed to

visit during his travels as a fly fisherman, he decided to attend. The conference literature offered little to help him understand what to expect, other than that there would be workshops, a concept he tried unsuccessfully to equate with what went on in a high school shop filled with teenagers and dangerous power tools. He studied maps and guidebooks and concluded that at the very least he could fish for trout in the evenings, perhaps only small fish in creeks, but when, Elgin asked himself, had he ever required more? On filling out his application Elgin also discovered the availability of fellowships for two students attending the conference, an award he immediately applied for, believing that, in this case, too, there existed an economy in which he should participate or prove himself a wastrel. He submitted two long poems in his fellowship application, "What Trout See" and "On the Theory and Practice of Love," a pair of recent poems that still delighted him when he reviewed them for submission, if only because the voice he heard while reading them seemed to belong to someone he would like to know and perhaps even fish with, although he worried, as well, that taken together the two poems might fail to earn him a fellowship because the theme of both poems was essentially the same.

His worries vanished on receipt of the notice announcing his fellowship. Elgin immediately set to work refashioning the contents of his small stream fly box, which he soon realized he had been neglecting of late as he grew more inclined to fish famous rivers throughout the West or, from September to the end of March, almost exclusively for steelhead. He enjoyed refilling the box with the simple, impressionistic patterns of his youth, the Adamses and Humpys, Hare's Ears and soft hackles, Stimulators and Trudes and Wulffs. The part of the process he liked most was scrutiny of the clean, organized composition of the completed box itself, the tidy rows of neatly stacked hairwings, the gradations in sizes for different patterns, the close quarters, the absence of unused space. Elgin also found himself unusually pleased by his own handiwork, evidence that after all these years his flies looked pretty, artful, effective—so unlike these same patterns tied, decades ago, when every fly he tied was for a small stream, the only kind of water he fished for trout, and no two flies turned out looking alike. Here was a box, he thought, carrying it upstairs from the basement to show his wife and daughters, that he could open on any stream anywhere and feel capable of catching trout. Here was work he was proud of.

He found his wife and two daughters, Erin and Alecka, in the living room with the television on. His wife sat at the far end of the leather sofa, wine glass in hand, her legs tucked under herself, the open bottle of Petite Syrah on the glass-topped end table. His daughters, who appeared to have simply collapsed on the carpet, spilling the contents of their school bags in a pattern that suggested, as well, a high-speed collision, were doing something to their nails that made it look as if they had slammed their hands in a car door. Elgin handed the open fly box to his wife and asked what she thought.

She knew what the flies were for. Elgin had spoken excitedly about the fishing he hoped to do while at the conference. His wife sipped from her glass, set it down, and tugged the hem of her gray flannel nightgown farther below her folded knees.

"I still can't believe you got a poetry scholarship," she announced, not unkindly, passing the fly box to their daughters.

"It's a fellowship," said Elgin, watching Alecka, the fourteen-year-old, hold the box as if something filthy might escape it. She rolled her eyes in the direction of her big sister.

"What's the difference?" asked his wife.

"I'm not sure," said Elgin. Did he just see Erin make the sign of the cross? "They're just different somehow."

"Well, it still seems weird," said Elgin's wife. Elgin took the fly box back from Erin, who immediately spun her hand around and examined her painfully colored nails at arm's length. "Didn't anyone else apply?"

Elgin checked to make sure the lid was snapped shut and then slid the fly box into a front pocket of his Levi's. He looked around the room for an opening in the drapes, wondering what the weather was doing.

"There's a second fellow, too."

Elgin stepped past his daughters and stood by the window, creating an equilateral triangle between him, his wife, and the television. Fellow sounded funny for a woman. He had never used the word like that. He parted the drapes with a finger, glancing out at the April night, imagining trout streams across the state stirring with spring.

"A woman, I think. Eudora Cromwell. The letter said I'm a fellow with someone named Eudora Cromwell."

Elgin's wife set down her wine glass and looked at him as if—no, he couldn't tell what her looks meant anymore. Elgin studied his wife and tried to recall what she looked like with all of her clothes off, with something in her hand she didn't keep putting between her lips. Then Elgin tried to decide if he could squeeze into the fly box in his pocket another half-dozen little Red Humpys along the foam left exposed by the tail-less soft hackles he had tied.

"You're going to write poetry with Dori Cromwell?" asked his wife.

"Write it; study it; work on it—something like that. I'm not a hundred percent sure."

"Did you hear that girls?"

Elgin's wife reached out and wrapped her hand around the neck of the wine bottle. Elgin was startled to note that his wife's gesture caused movement next to the fly box in his pocket.

"Your father's going to write poems with Dori Cromwell."

Erin and Alecka looked up at Elgin, waving their fingers to help their nail polish dry.

49

◦◦

*Ten thousand days afield,* thinks Dori Cromwell—a line from her own poem, titled the same, that appeared in her first and only book, the celebrated and oft-reprinted collection, *Slate Blue.*

She can't recall the next line. She feels it someplace in her mind— or perhaps it's on the page itself she can almost see it. She isn't sure which. She steps back from her Subaru, its bright body radiating heat from the afternoon sun, and she wonders if it's finally true, maybe now she really has spent that many days finding sport outdoors— maybe today, this very day, that poem is true.

Or tomorrow, thinks Dori Cromwell.

She finishes ministering her aging skin, protecting it with the same care she had given the skin of her children, covering every inch of her exposed flesh with sunblock purchased from a Costa Rican naturopath online. Nearby, the river murmurs gently beyond a road-side reach of scrub oak and stunted Ponderosa pine, the Grande Ronde, the Minam, the Wallowa, she isn't sure where they are. No matter, she thinks, glad, just glad to be outdoors again, afield, no matter how many days she's been here—on rivers, on mountains, on beaches, on boats, preparing herself, readying herself, coloring her-self with some magic potion as if a warrior preparing for battle, an image that delights her as the thought of candy, she imagines, might delight a child.

"What is that shit?"

Elgin Fischer, looking over at Dori, finishes knotting the laces of his dusty sneakers.

"Smells like a French whorehouse."

Dori grins, a wave of relief passing through her body. Afield or not, she had started to wonder if this trip with Elgin Fischer was a good idea. He didn't even bring his fishing gear, for Christ's sake. For four hours Elgin sat squirming in the passenger seat, asking her about her husband, her work, her grown-up kids, her new house, her newest car, never once allowing the conversation to turn to him, never once talking the way she remembered about fishing, poetry, about language, about life—never once offering her a glimpse of the mind of the man whose company ten years ago at the writing conference they are headed to now had sparked a period of creativity, unprecedented and unmatched since, that ended upon completion of *Slate Blue*.

The word *shit* put her at ease.

"Have you ever been to France, Elgin?" asks Dori.

"Of course not."

Elgin holds out a hand and she squeezes a dollop of sunblock on the back of it.

"I've never even been to Florida."

She watches Elgin scrub the lotion into his hands, the honey-colored skin on the back of them covered with freckles, faint age spots, scars, the skin wrinkled, undulant with bone and vein, hands, thinks Dori—a thought she fails to carry forward beyond the single word.

"Have you ever paid for a prostitute?" she asks.

Elgin tugs on his floppy fishing hat, the only gear—besides sunglasses—he brought along. She studies him, hoping he'll tell her the truth, having no reason to suspect he won't, other than her own inability of late to know the truth, to delineate her self and her life from poetry, from the relentless ironies of language and art.

"No. I haven't."

Elgin takes up her rod, left leaning against the Subaru, and tucks it at the reel under his arm. He removes his sunglasses, lowers them from the corkie around his neck, and replaces his reading glasses and adjusts the second corkie behind him.

"Might've been better off if I had." Elgin looks again at her over the tops of his glasses, an old man look, she thinks. Yet his eyes are bright and blue, studying her between the frames of his glasses and the wavy brim of his hat—and the fact is, she recalls, he's nearly five years younger than she is.

"Could've saved me a lot of heartache," he adds, shrugging his shoulders—a gesture so submissive it angers Dori.

"What about love, Elgin?"

Dori throws him a look, trying to contain it, keep it from spilling over into the frustration she's felt of late trying to write.

"Or you telling me that's all love is?"

Elgin unhooks the bushy fly from the stripping guide. He frees the loop of leader from around the reel and lets the line hang while he dresses the fly with floatant he found in her pack with her other gear. He puts the floatant back in a pocket of his shorts and returns the leader and fly to how they were.

"Even a trout would know there's more to it than that—if a trout had a brain big enough to know anything at all."

This time Elgin shrugs with his eyebrows—same movement, same pace, same gesture—and the recognition of this likeness between the up-and-down of Elgin's expressive shoulders and his gray, owly brows disarms Dori with the force of a drug taken directly up her nose.

"There's always more to it," says Elgin, his gaze drifting off in the direction of the river. "Just like fishing."

"You can say that about anything, Elgin."

"I think I already did. Or is that something you wrote?"

She's sure Elgin doesn't expect a reply. Nor does Dori remind Elgin that, ten years ago, he did say that, he wrote it, too, a line from one of the two poems he submitted for his fellowship and read, at the end of their week together, to an overflow audience he made laugh and cry and, upon finish, stand and applaud in a way she has never since heard an audience respond, despite the untold number of standing ovations she has received over the years on reading from *Slate Blue* to houses large and small. Worse, thinks Dori, certain as well she won't remind him of this, either, she used the same line in a poem of her own, "On the Theory and Practice of Flyfishing," repeating it at the end of each stanza in a poem included in *Slate Blue*, a book which, more and more, seems to her a direct result of the week she spent upriver from here, wherever they are, with this odd man, this unschooled poet named Elgin Fischer.

She did put the line—each time—in quotation marks, Dori tells herself. Wasn't that enough? Near him now, at ease with him again, relishing the odd, visceral sensation of her mind close to his, she recalls writing the poems in *Slate Blue* directly to Elgin Fischer, as if he were sitting there listening to her, responding to her, laughing and smiling and sometimes tearing up and gazing off in that way he had when moved by hard things that seemed just beneath the surface of whatever he saw, some shadow that made his enthusiasm and excitement all the more poignant, more vibrant, more inviting to share. Why shouldn't she have quoted, in one small poem, Elgin Fischer's exact words? Dori asks herself, aiming her key at the locks of her Subaru. And why, following their reading together, shouldn't she have led him to her room and made love with him throughout the long, celebrative night?

Still, Dori Cromwell recognizes her capacity for self-deceit. Nothing about the phrase—"just like fishing"—couldn't have been hers or someone else's words, created independent from Elgin Fischer's poem or ideas or enthusiastic appetite for sex. Yet she immediately dismisses even this defense as but a veiled attempt to introduce chance, fate, or even irony, when what she feels she is dealing with, more and more, is fraudulent work—or, worse, the complete loss of herself as an artist if not also a woman with anything inside her she recognizes as a heart.

Dori moves off after Elgin. He leads her along the edge of the highway, looking somehow like an oversized elf in his sunglasses, gray beard and silly hat, T-shirt and baggy green shorts riding low on his hipless butt. Or is it buttless hips, thinks Dori—and she smiles, startled by the question, the odd turn of phrase. *Elgin Fischer*, she thinks, italics and all, certain she looks pretty silly, too, and hoping maybe, just maybe, she was right after all inviting him to join her.

"This oughta do," says Elgin, starting down a break in the underbrush. "Wherever there's a trail, there's a fishing hole."

Once again Dori wonders if this is a line from Elgin's poetry, if he's quoting himself, or is it something so simple about fishing—and the world—that everybody knows it.

Everybody but her.

"Do we need to worry about poison oak here?" she asks.

Elgin stops halfway down the short steep trail and holds up a hand for her.

"I don't think so. Rattlesnakes, maybe. But no poison oak."

Before she can decide if he's joking or not, she catches Elgin glancing at her bare legs.

"You know, Elgin, I don't care if we catch anything." She takes his arm just below the shoulder, allows him to place his hand high on hers. "I just want to cool off, get a casting lesson."

Elgin guides her over exposed rocks embedded in the dusty trail. He stops at water's edge.

"You think you don't care," he says, handing her the rod. "But it's more fun if we do."

Fun, however, has long ceased to seem significant in Dori Cromwell's life.

When *Slate Blue* was finally published, three years after her week-long fellowship with Elgin Fischer, Dori felt relief more than anything else, a sense of vindication for all that she had given up to accomplish the work. Socialite, actress and model, editor, broadcaster, publisher, mother and wife, grandmother and teacher and fundraiser—what in God's name was the point of Dori writing poetry, asked family and friends, when she had so much else to show for her life, that peculiar blend of material, emotional, and spiritual balance that Americans believe a national if not constitutional right.

Her husband, the magnate Vincent Buhr, proved most perplexed by his then new wife's literary ambitions. He understood, as well as anyone, the need to create, to express oneself, to rise through the ranks and discover what one is made of. His fortune, he believed, was evidence of his understanding of his wife's drive, her intense desire to write what she described, simply, as good poetry.

Still, two years after Dori Cromwell became his wife, and her slender book of poems was well received by critics and public alike, when the reception to her book earned her appearances on national morning television, attention in newspapers and magazines and what she made him to understand were the important literary journals, when *Slate Blue* received that startling nomination for a National Book Award, when Dori was invited to read and teach and receive handsome fees for attending conferences worldwide, when all of this happened over the course of the early, easy years of their marriage, Vincent Buhr thought that might be it, Dori had done what she set out to do, she had proven something immeasurably significant to her and him and her grown-up children from her distant first marriage, to everyone else in her remarkable life, and now, thought Buhr, this would be the end of it, the last of her wild dream to create something that, really, few people anywhere actually read, something, unfortunately, that would never create a job, never feed a hungry mouth, stop a disease, or end a war—even if somebody could understand, thought Buhr, half of what Dori's poems might be about.

Still, over time, Vincent Buhr felt he could live with the mystery—as long as he got what he needed out of his marriage, as long as Dori was happy, too.

Is she? Vincent Buhr looks distractedly out the cabin of *Slate Blue*, the pretty R44 Raven he bought shortly after publication of his wife's book of poetry, a gesture he still feels demonstrates the care and understanding he has brought to their years together. No matter, he thinks, that he's always owned and flown helicopters, a thought that brings to mind a flurry of ships all the way back to the Huey he flew clearing out Saigon, when he barely had hair on his ass. No matter, he thinks, watching the kid in a Mariner's cap handling the fuel line out in the heat, that his willingness to hang his neck out in these frigging machines has gone a long way to make him as rich as he is, whether he named them *Moby Dick* or *Pussy Galore*. No matter, thinks Vincent Buhr—sitting in some Podunk airfield in—where is he?—La Grande, Oregon—that *Slate Blue*, like everything else in his life, is about making his life work. No matter, thinks Vincent, waving the kid off and reaching for the magneto switch, that little else in his life has proven more effective than a tool that helps him get around, get around fast, scout new property, and keep track of what he already owns.

Is Dori happy? Vincent asks himself, holding the question as the engine fires, while he waits for the head temp to rise, checks the hydraulics in the collective. Happy as a pig in shit, thinks Vincent, picturing his wife yammering away all weekend about poetry, about writing and words, about art, about life, all the usual high-minded crap she said she needed to talk about with that little flyfishing prick, Elgin Fischer.

All during run-up, engine instruments each creeping toward green, Vincent Buhr recalls the occasion, years before, when Dori returned long past midnight to their vacation home on the Deschutes River Ranch after an evening supposedly spent fishing with Elgin Fischer. The memory starts again in a spot directly behind Vincent's belt buckle, spreads once more into his stomach, up his back, into his shoulders and arms, a sudden flu-like ache that he knows is more than anger and shame, jealousy, sadness, disgust. Two a.m. by the time Dori finally entered their bedroom—and Vincent could smell the champagne and God knows what else on her, the scent of her filling the room, bringing to mind the last elk he shot after exhausting it, surreptitiously, following pursuit up a remote Ochoco canyon in *Slate Blue.*

"Where you been?" he asked, rolling over in bed as Dori made directly for her bathroom. She left the door open, dropped her clothes to the floor, wrapped herself in the robe left lying on the edge of the marble tub. At the sink she ran water into her hands, talked to him while washing her face, her neck, her eyes.

"On the river. With Elgin Fischer. Where I said I'd be."

Vincent watched Dori run her fingers inside a jar and work something into her skin.

"Kind of dark to fish, isn't it?"

Dori stood in the doorway brushing her teeth.

"Elgin fixed dinner. He brought his camp gear. And champagne. To celebrate poetry."

Closing the throttle, checking that the main rotor and engine rpm needles split accordingly, Vincent recalls rolling over, turning his back toward Dori, the same ache he's feeling now twisting him away from her. He felt her sit down on her side of the bed, turned to see her back to him.

"'S the matter, Vincent? You jealous?"

Vincent reached out a hand. He hung a finger over the belt around Dori's waist, tugging gently.

"Of a fucking poet?" he said. And soon as he did, Vincent recognized he had made the biggest mistake of his marriage.

Dori's back rose and fell as she took a deep breath inside her robe. Then she moved herself just enough that Vincent had to let go of the belt unless he wanted to force it loose.

"I was just worried about you," he tried, placing his hand on the small of Dori's back. "That's a big river. Something could happen."

"I'm careful, Vincent. You know that."

Dori opened her robe, let it fall to the floor, and slid under the covers.

"I've always been careful."

Vincent moved toward her. He let a hand rest lightly on her hip.

"Well, you never know," he said, sensing everything would be okay, the line about poets wasn't going to ruin the night after all. "I'm up in the Raven tomorrow and something weird happens. That's it. You just never know."

Needles matched again, governor switched on, engine and rotor rpm in operating range, Vincent remembers sliding his hand onto Dori's stomach.

"You can always stay on the ground, Vincent," she said. "It's not like you need anything you don't already have."

Then Dori backed herself close to him, and Vincent wrapped his arm around her and drew her tight.

"What about you, Dori?"

Dori took his arm and adjusted it, keeping her breasts to herself.

"What *about* me?" she said.

Vincent Buhr makes one last check to see everything in the green, all warning lights out, and the Raven lifts into its hover. He knows damn well his wife isn't happy. But what he doesn't know, what he only suspects or intuits, his insides aching, is that the high aims he and Dori Cromwell once brought to their marriage have conspired to produce in his wife, seven years after publication of *Slate Blue*, a state of near numbness, her only feeling of late a gnawing sense of starvation, as if she is living off old toast and dried fruit—enough, maybe, to keep her alive, but she can feel parts of herself grown weak from malnutrition, her mind and heart atrophied at the edges, this insidious numbness creeping ever deeper into her, whoever she is, a discovery she fights daily to make as she faces the blank page.

Unknown to her husband, the astute and famously successful Vincent Buhr, Dori Cromwell is aching to piece together another volume of poetry that will satisfy a ferocious desire to be embraced by the ten-thousand-year-old guild of poets, to view herself as worthy of membership, on her own merits, of a lasting place among the voices remembered for a manner of artistry that nothing else in her fabulous life can remotely satisfy.

❧

Vincent, of course, could publish her next book, thinks Dori, as she often does, this time while one step away from the river, feeling the delicate touch of Elgin Fischer's hand around her naked bicep. She doesn't quite hate her husband for that power, for that kind of foolproof, flip-of-the-switch pragmatism he brings to their lovemaking, for the power he feels he possesses to move the deal—any deal—forward. But the feeling has left her in a state of imbalance for as long as she can remember, as though her feet, or center of gravity, have lost contact with the earth. Vincent could pay for a run of a half-million copies, thinks Dori, with spare change from the cookie jar.

"Careful," says Elgin, easing her off the last of the dry cobble at river's edge. "Those shoes of yours look slippery."

"And this one feels loose," says Dori, stopping suddenly, freeing her arm from Elgin's grip and gesturing toward the bottom of her leg next to his.

She hands him the rod, bends to retie her shoe. Elgin, she notes, averts his eyes again. He steps into the river, bends forward himself, and lifts a rock from the water, examining it. Dori closes her eyes, feeling the sun on the backs of her calves. All of this, she recognizes, is foolish. She knows what a dangerous weight she's attached to both the past and the present, that the mere consideration of a single collection of early poems as anything more than a lucky shot in the dark has been reckless, if not artistically suicidal. She can't help herself. She has taken to glorifying her life and past work to ridiculous, mythological proportions. Her ego, she feels, has metastasized—leaving her

59

both starved and numb except for this angry desire to create another volume of poetry, poems she can't possibly write, she fears now more than ever, without the help of Elgin Fischer.

"Ready?"

Elgin stands knee-deep in the river, rod tucked under his arm, not looking at her even though he just spoke, turning over another rock in his hands, examining it as if it's a book he were just handed and asked to read, the hem of his shorts already wet, as if he can't wait, thinks Dori, he's going fishing with or without her. She sees it's crazy; she's crazy. For a moment she pictures herself standing in a doorway, embracing the wonder of all that brought her to this threshold, where she awaits her next step into the mystery ahead. Elgin Fischer, her muse?

Why not, she concludes, stepping into the river, cool water gripping her ankles.

ᖇ

Once in the river, Elgin Fischer finally relaxes. Cold water draws the heat from him, a thermal capillary action that settles his heart, allowing him to breathe deeply, evenly, for the first time in hours. Turning rocks to look at bugs—mayfly nymphs, caddis larvae—he glances repeatedly from behind his sunglasses at Dori Cromwell, wondering what he's doing here with a gal like her. Let him fall in love again, he thinks, knowing he's already halfway there. A lot of good that will do him.

"Look at this," he offers, anyway, stepping back to Dori's side.

He shows her the difference between the various mayfly nymphs and a pair of stoneflies—Little Yellow Sallies—that he's surprised haven't yet hatched, and two different types of cases that caddis make. This close to her, he can smell her, despite the lotion, and he wonders how much of this smell is just her, the heat, or if, like him, she's affected by their proximity. He returns the rock to the river, hands Dori the rod.

"We have the right fly?" she asks, taking his arm.

"Not even close," says Elgin. He begins moving carefully along the edge of the soft current, his feet slipping into place between the rocks, speaking while he wades: "We're just going to give them something that looks real, something good enough to eat. A river like this, trout aren't very sophisticated. Something big and bold catches their attention. Long as it floats naturally, they can't help themselves. They're hardwired to rise."

Elgin stops, recognizing how much he's suddenly talking. He positions them just downstream from a little seam and narrow run that looks as good as any spot he's seen on this short piece of water. He tells Dori to free the fly. For a moment she just stands there, smiling at him.

"Elgin, why is it everything you say about fishing sounds like innuendo, like you could just as well be talking about sex?"

Elgin tilts his head forward, pulling his sunglasses to the end of his nose. He holds Dori's gaze for several moments and then pushes his glasses back tight to his eyes.

"Probably because I could be," he says, taking the rod from Dori. He unhooks the Humpy, clears the leader knot through the tip guide. "Seems to me," he adds, gesturing with an abrupt sweep of the rod, "this whole thing's wired up the same."

Elgin makes several short, harsh casts, forcing line out the end of the rod. Then he turns square to Dori, his front to her side, and he wraps an arm around her, takes her by the wrist, and inserts the rod grip correctly in the palm of her hand.

"Of course," says Elgin, "I don't pay attention to much else but what happens in the wet spots between the banks."

"Gimme a break, Elgin," says Dori, allowing him to steady her while she casts.

❦

It is only later, much later, that Elgin Fischer considers the significance of the enormous mayfly, a Big Yellow May, *Hexagenia limbata*, that lighted near the river on the pile of Dori Cromwell's green summer dress. In Elgin's experience, the Hex hatch had always been confined to lakes and slow meandering rivers and streams, and only those that offer silty bottoms that the Hex nymphs require to burrow and live before emerging on the edge of summer nights.

"They're not usually from this kind of spot," said Elgin, lifting the mayfly, yellow as a canary, by its impressive, veiny wings. "Of course it may not even be from this river. They fly. Wind can take them anywhere. That's a lot different, I guess, than fish."

"Maybe we can't compare everything to fish and fishing," said Dori, running a hand toward the mayfly up Elgin's bare, sweaty arm.

Elgin recalls tossing the mayfly, big as a grasshopper, into the air. Then he handed Dori her clothing, enjoying another look at her healthy, responsive body. They both began to dress, remembers Elgin, when they were stunned by the roar of Vincent Buhr's helicopter, *Slate Blue*, sweeping up the river as if the mayfly, the hex, transformed by the Muses themselves.

"That's Vincent!" said Dori, trying to cover herself, a blast of wind tearing at the dress in her hands.

"How do you know?" asked Elgin, shouting to be heard over the thunder of the approaching blades.

"How do I know?" cried Dori, her voice beyond anything he had ever imagined.

Yet it's that single, displaced mayfly, big and yellow as the midday sun, that returns to trouble Elgin most. Time and again he fails to rid himself of the notion of some terrible connection between the events that followed, as if Vincent Buhr himself, by some strange twisted

62

power, had been induced by that lone mayfly to strike, just as the ten-inch rainbow, sometime before, was brought to the surface of the river, fooled by Dori's cast and bushy yellow fly—just as Elgin himself had finally struck, as it were, when, on a grassy bank downstream from where she had caught her trout, Dori Cromwell, astride him the first time, spurred him to ecstasy beneath the hem of her summer dress.

Just where did that mayfly come from? Elgin asks himself, over and over, and just why did it light on Dori's dress, tossed aside, later, next to them?

The rest, as was soon said, is history.

*five*

# The River Beulah

Instead of adding on that year they parked a double-wide on top of cinder blocks in a corner of the playground. They must have decided to do it just before school started, because you could tell right off it was a rush job, with the blocks out in the open and the stairs and wheelchair ramp made out of pressure-treated two-by-fours, gun nails all around, not a deck screw in sight. By the time students arrived one of the posts under the landing had already sunk into the asphalt, softened by the sun, so that every time you walked into Mr. Fairchild's room you felt as if the door—and everything inside—was slightly skewed.

He must have been a rush job, too. With the prison going in we suddenly had more families and kids in the valley than anybody knew what to do with. They had added classrooms the year before but somebody must have miscalculated the appeal of government jobs and contracts. Either that or the number of criminals in the state, my mom said. She and her family had been in the valley forever, so even though she was raising me alone she was on the school board, which is how she had her eye on Mr. Fairchild from the start.

Not that she would have had anything to do with hiring him. The school board position meant she had friends, which brings with it its own kind of power, but not the kind that decides who kids spend time with in a classroom. But maybe the kind of power that decides who they *don't* spend time with. I'm not sure about that. I do know that kind of power exists, although where it comes from—or even what it is—is anybody's guess.

I don't know, either, if Mr. Fairchild took a job here just because he found one, or if he really did hope to spend the rest of his career where he could fish a river, as he said, until his dying days. No doubt the man liked his time on the water. But that's a clear kind of power, one that pretty much everyone in the valley agrees on. And you don't have to cast flies to understand it, although that never hurt anyone I ever knew of.

Mr. Fairchild let us sit wherever we wanted the first day. I came in out of the hard sunlight hitting that crooked-seeming door and had to stop a second to let my eyes adjust. Lisa Mullins was already front and center, where she sat in every class we were given a choice. I went up to join her, like I usually did, my footsteps loud on the hollow floor. Not that we were boyfriend and girlfriend or anything like that. Lisa Mullins and I had grown up together, that's all, and I was still young enough to believe a guy like me had a chance, somewhere down the road, with a girl like her.

She had on a sleeveless button-up blouse, a white one like lots of girls wore that year, with black pants that went down below her knees with little slits along the sides of her calves. I had seen my mother in the same style of blouse and pants for as long as I could remember, so I was sure it was nothing new, all the way down to the steep slip-ons with the tall heels that looked like they were made out of wraps of thin manila rope. But the style looked good on Lisa. Everything did.

Just before Mr. Fairchild got started a new kid by the name of Prather sat down at the desk on the other side of Lisa. That evening at dinner my mom said he was the son of somebody important at the prison, a father whose wife was still somewhere back in California. She looked out of the top of her eyes when she said it, a look that meant I ought to be able to understand what was really going on. But when the new kid took the other seat next to Lisa all I knew was his name from the period before, and the way he kept looking at her as though he could see right through the part of her blouse held together by the buttons below the two she had left undone.

"Let's begin."

Mr. Fairchild started in without warning. We didn't know it yet, but they never did get a bell in his classroom. It wasn't long, of course, before kids started straggling in late, making the usual lame excuses, although I'll hand it to Mr. Fairchild, he always began on time, whether students were ready or not. Even when things got hard for him, he went by the rules. He showed up and tried to teach us that there was more to the world than Albion, the valley, and the River Beulah. He tried to get us to understand that the world didn't end at the horizon.

Yet that first day all he could talk about was how glad he was to be here teaching at our high school, how lucky he felt to have landed a job in a place blessed with so many fine people, so much good country, magnificent scenery, and a river where wild fish still spawned as they had for thousands and thousands of years. The Beulah seemed to have made the biggest impression on him. The Beulah and its steelhead. Did we know how lucky we were? he asked. Most of us, I imagined, did. Listening to Mr. Fairchild talk excitedly about this place that many of us had always called home, it was easy to believe that whatever else was happening in the world, we were safe in the valley, free of the troubles that seemed to grow everywhere else year by year. Here is a man, I remember thinking, who has seen that world. We are lucky, I thought, and for more reasons than this excited old guy would ever know.

I wasn't the only one impressed. Lisa followed him back and forth across the front of the low-ceilinged room with her friendly eyes, blue that day as the dry September sky. Her hand rose innocently to her neck, and for a moment I watched the tips of her fingers moving back and forth between the two unused buttons. Later, I glanced over at her again and saw the third button undone. At the same instant I caught the gaze of the new kid Prather looking directly where I had just been looking. His eyes met mine and he raised his eyebrows, smiling obscenely.

I looked away and discovered Mr. Fairchild watching the three of us, his gaze taking in what had just happened. Or at least the part between me and Prather. Yet I had to believe he noticed that open button as well, if not the act, conscious or otherwise, of Lisa undoing it, then at least the result of that act, the deepening V of white against that much more of her exposed skin. Mr. Fairchild stood silently in front of the class, his eyes studying the three of us and no one else— as if waiting for a response to a question he had asked.

I raised my hand. It was bad enough he had caught me looking down Lisa Mullins' blouse, but he had also seen, I was sure, the smile that Prather gave me. I wanted to make sure Mr. Fairchild, the new teacher, didn't think I was that kind of kid—or at least that I wasn't pals with a guy like Prather and his leering smile.

"So where did you used to teach?" I asked.

Mr. Fairchild smiled. He had deep wrinkles at the corners of his eyes, and his skin was rough and splotchy, as if he had worked out-doors too much earlier in his life. But his eyes were as blue as Lisa's, a color that made him look younger than he probably was, and there was always a strange light in them, as if he were about to tell us all a secret or a good joke.

"Oh, I've taught all over the place," he said. "Up and down the coast. In the cities. Other states. California, mostly."

"What brought you to Albion?" Lisa spoke without raising her hand, as if this was already another class where, inevitably, she became buddies with the teacher. Mr. Fairchild didn't seem to mind. He looked directly at her, as though she were the only one in the room.

"Just this job. The last school I was at was having problems with enrollment. Of course as a fly fisherman I already knew about the Beulah, so when I heard about the opening here I applied. Certainly beats California."

"Bullshit."

Mr. Fairchild looked a moment longer at Lisa Mullins before turning to Prather, who had spoken the obscenity as casually as clearing his throat. Whether that moment Mr. Fairchild took was to steal a glance down Lisa's unbuttoned blouse, we'll never know. I wouldn't have blamed him. Mr. Fairchild meant a lot of different things to a lot of different people in this valley, but he taught me one thing, and that's that people are no different wherever you go. They make mistakes. They do silly things. They do bad things, too, one time or another in their lives. Whether or not Mr. Fairchild did anything wrong here remains anybody's guess. All I know for sure is people made it impossible for him to stay, and he did the right thing getting out when he could still leave like a man.

By "people" I mean the likes of Prather, Prather's father, all the other people who couldn't handle Mr. Fairchild standing up to them, and everybody else who believed that Lisa Mullins wasn't capable of undoing another button just to see what kind of power she really had in this world, people like my mother and maybe even me. For I admit I was one of them, somebody else who didn't come to Mr. Fairchild's defense, if only to get up and tell a punk like new kid Prather to shut up and treat a teacher with respect, leave the tough guy act to prison, the locker room, Saturday night—or California.

But I didn't do anything. Neither did Mr. Fairchild. He finished looking at Lisa Mullins and then he turned to Prather and waited for him to say more. Or that's what it seemed like. Mr. Fairchild stood there gazing patiently at Prather, giving no indication that he was bothered in the least by what had just been said. I heard Kyle Peterson snicker toward the back of the room, but I cut my eyes at him to make him stop right now.

Finally, Prather spoke again. "You know you're telling us what a great place this is? Well I think it sucks. This is nowhere, man. The only thing around is a damn prison."

"Maybe you ought to try fishing."

That got everybody laughing. Everybody but Prather. Mr. Fairchild looked around the room, pleased with the reaction he had gotten with so little effort. I think everybody needed to let out a little air. None of us was used to this kind of tension in a classroom.

"Yeah, right," said Prather, holding his mouth like he had just sucked on something sour. "My dad says the only thing coming to this valley anymore is pure scum. He says everybody knows the fishing and everything else in this valley has gone to hell. Why else would they put a prison here?"

"Anything else?" asked Mr. Fairchild. Prather looked over at me and Lisa Mullins. We both turned away, giving our attention back to Mr. Fairchild.

"Thank you for sharing," he said.

The first fish Mr. Fairchild brought over for my mother to cook must have run about five or six pounds, not a particularly big fish although that didn't seem to be the point. By then we could only keep hatchery fish anyway, and most of the summer-runs had taken on that same-

70

ness of size and configuration that you see in trees in planted forests and trout in stocked lakes. Still, no one doubted what it meant for such a fish to have gone to the sea and returned, and Mr. Fairchild was excited to share the story of how he had teased the fish to the surface with a waking fly, as though, listening to him, you would have thought he was some sort of snake charmer.

I heard all about it while my mother put the fish in the oven after opening bottles of beer for Mr. Fairchild and herself. I was used to guys coming by now and then for dinner, but it took me a while to figure out that there had been talk between Mr. Fairchild and my mother at some start-of-school function, and he had joked about bringing by a fish sometime if he ever caught one. I got this from both sides, Mr. Fairchild in our so-called living room, my mother in the kitchen just big enough for one person to turn around in. I sat on one of the bar stools at the counter that divided the front half of our apartment, our house as long as I could remember or at least since my father left way back when.

All of this seems important now because it explains why I wasn't very talkative when Mr. Fairchild started asking me questions. The idea was that I was keeping our guest company while my mother got dinner ready in the kitchen. But she was right there. We didn't have a real house. We didn't have a real kitchen. Yet that never stopped my mother from acting like we did. Mr. Fairchild asked me all the usual questions—how I liked school, sports I played, work, girl-friends, plans for the future—but I didn't open up much, not with my mother listening even if I had felt like talking.

We ate right there at the counter, my mother going into her room to bring out the stool she used for tying flies. She worked at a tall drafting table she got for free from the high school, and she was always proud of that stool because the day she bought it was the day, she said, she stopped working for anybody else. When she came out from her room I noticed she had run a brush through her hair and let down the sleeves of the blouse she had kept clean under an apron while she was cooking.

"Another beer?" she asked.

Mr. Fairchild said he didn't mind. My mother was never what you would call a serious drinker, but she liked her beer and wine and she had the kind of figure that could handle a little softness around the edges. I've no doubt Mr. Fairchild noticed that, too. Like most likable people, he paid attention to you, showing more interest in you than himself. The way things work in this world, that same quality, that gift he had, is probably the same exact thing that caused him so much trouble. That's an awfully strange notion but there you have it. My mother got something from Mr. Fairchild, and she thought she deserved it at the exclusion of anyone else.

Not long after this, Lisa Mullins asked Mr. Fairchild to teach her how to fly fish. I don't know when exactly she asked him, just one day at the start of class Mr. Fairchild came up to me and told me about it and said he would consider such a request if I came along as well.

I was confused by Lisa's eagerness to learn. It seemed unlikely a girl who had never been to the river to do more than get a suntan or drink a six-pack with friends would find much to enjoy in fly fishing. I understood the attraction to Mr. Fairchild, but that kind of thing wears off pretty quickly after a few hundred casts and humping it from one run to the next.

I also thought Mr. Fairchild would be taking a big chance, even with me along. The thing you have to understand in a valley like this is that the girls are always right. They may act stupid, they may do silly or even dumb things, but they're still always right, anything that goes wrong is the guy's fault. At least that's the way it always seemed to me.

So I was worried from the start what could happen to Lisa on the river and the trouble that would bring Mr. Fairchild's way. I'm talking about anything. She stubs her toe, she gets a fly caught in her ear, Mr. Fairchild's in the hot seat. Of course what I was really worried about was a lot worse.

I even told my mother. She shrugged her shoulders, hunched though they were over the vise, as if to say what Lisa Mullins and Mr. Fairchild did was none of her damn business. Then she broke her thread. She was cinching up on the head of a fly, some kind of bead-head nymph from what I could see. She cussed and turned around and looked at me.

"Anything else?"

Still, I went along. More than once, too, and each time Lisa got a little better, straightening her line behind her, putting the fly on the water in a way that might fool a fish if she ever swung it by one. Mr. Fairchild was a good teacher. He was patient, and he liked to talk about how to do things, what he thought while trying to do them. I learned a little bit, too, although mostly I would take off on my own because I figured if we were going fishing, I was there to fish.

One evening just before daylight savings ended I got a fish to move at the bottom of a big tailout that was so slow I could barely get the fly to swing. The fish showed itself once with a slow, lazy roll that might have seemed like it didn't have anything to do with what I was doing if I didn't know better. But it's always you and the fly, I believe. I went through all my flies, all my ideas, all my different casts and swings and hunches and twice more the fish came up to the surface although never with any real heart. But it was enough to keep me interested and I kept on trying pretty much until dark.

Back at Mr. Fairchild's truck I first thought I must have missed them somewhere back on the river where we had started in. Then I saw the two of them sitting in the cab, Mr. Fairchild's hands moving around like they did when he explained something. I put my rod in back and pulled off my waders, trying to keep my mind on what I might have done differently to fool that pissant steelhead. Coming

73

up along the side of the truck I saw the window go down and Lisa stuck out her head.

"Hop in, stranger! We thought you'd never get back!"

It all got even more confusing after that. Time changed, which meant there was practically no daylight to fish after school, and then my mom said I couldn't go fishing any longer with Mr. Fairchild, Lisa Mullins or no Lisa Mullins. I asked her why. She said that was her own business, that as a mother raising a teenage boy she didn't need to explain. I'd heard that enough to know where it would get me arguing and, anyway, by then it had started to rain in earnest and it looked like it would be awhile before anybody did much fishing.

But I guess Mr. Fairchild stayed at it. Not long before Thanksgiving he called my mother one Friday after school and said he had another fish he'd like to bring over. At first my mom refused, making up an excuse about needing to finish a big order for a shop in Seattle. Then she stood listening and nodding her head and finally smiling as Mr. Fairchild must have gone on and on the way he could, even if it was only about fishing. Pretty soon my mom even laughed, although I watched her shake her head as she did, as if Mr. Fairchild got her to laugh at something she still didn't agree with, or the way she might if I spilled something and said something funny and she was feeling like life wasn't so bad after all.

Mr. Fairchild stayed late that night. He and my mom drank the beer he brought, and then my mom pulled out one of the bottles of wine she always kept in the cabinet above the refrigerator for a special occasion. I finally went to bed, which didn't put me far from the action, but then I finally drifted off, as I often did back then, thinking about a fish, this time the one that Mr. Fairchild brought over, and all that had to have happened for it to find its way into our lives.

In the morning everybody at school was upset. Lisa Mullins hadn't come home that night. Neither had the new kid Prather. The two of them had gone out on some sort of date, although what that meant in the valley wouldn't have been a whole lot. Mr. Fairchild looked a mess. The night with my mom appeared to have about done him in. He had us read extra long from our novels, and then he put in a video and turned out the lights. When the cops came they talked to Mr. Fairchild out on the landing with the door open, their voices quiet beneath the sound of the movie and a steady rain.

When I got home from school my mom said they had suspended Mr. Fairchild until investigations of the disappearance of two Albion High School students were completed. There was something they didn't like about his story. He had explained to the police that he had eaten dinner with my mother at our house and that he had stayed until around midnight and then gone home. The cops came by and questioned my mom. She said that was right, although it might have been a little earlier that Mr. Fairchild left, more like eleven, she thought, since he had gone home right after they got done watching the news.

But then they asked her about a small box of steelhead flies that they had found in Lisa Mullins' bedroom. My mom said she had given the flies to Mr. Fairchild that evening. She said she gave them to him as thanks for the nice fish he brought us for dinner. She was sure they were the same flies, and that she had tied them herself. How could she not recognize her own work?

But Mr. Fairchild couldn't explain how Lisa Mullins ended up with the flies. Or how they ended up in her bedroom. Or he wouldn't explain. All he said was that he had had quite a bit to drink with my mother and he must have left the fly box on the seat of his car when he got home. Had he locked his car? the cops asked. Mr. Fairchild said he couldn't remember.

"Conveniently," said my mom. She looked at me out of the tops of her eyes. "That's what they always say. 'I don't remember.' When what's obvious what happened is your friend Mr. Fairchild got a little excited over here and decided to pay a visit to his fly fishing student Lisa Mullins. That's what happened. At least that's the start of it. Where she is now, God help us."

"How can you say that! I thought you liked Mr. Fairchild!"

"Chet, I know. Mr. Fairchild wasn't exactly a gentleman after you went to bed last night. I suspect we both had a little too much to drink. And I can't say I didn't resist some of his advances. But I know where to draw the line. I guess your friend Mr. Fairchild doesn't know how to take no for an answer."

"I can't believe it," I said.

"Believe it, Chet. They found the flies. In her bedroom. Don't you see? We don't even know the man. We don't know his past. He just showed up here. That's the way they work."

"The way *who* works?" I demanded.

"Guys like Mr. Fairchild."

I knew it was all lies, people trying to make up something to help them feel better about something they couldn't make sense of. I'm not saying Mr. Fairchild was harmless. Or not guilty of things. You teach people to look at the world and some of them are going to lose their innocence and that makes the teacher somehow responsible. There's a price to learning.

But I know he was innocent of the charges made against him. I know that because Lisa Mullins called me that night. She called while my mother was at the meeting about Mr. Fairchild's fate in Albion, talking in a funny squeaky voice until she was sure it was me who had picked up the phone. She and Prather were on their way to California. She just called, she said, to say goodbye to me and, if I would do it, Mr. Fairchild.

"Why him?" I asked.

"What do you mean, why? Because he helped me get out of Albion. He helped me leave. He tried to help all of us. You know that."

"Why don't you call him yourself?"

"I can't, Chet. I'd get him in trouble. Or he'd turn me in. He'd have to. He's a teacher."

"Not any more. Not in Albion. They're meeting right now to can his ass. He'll be lucky if he doesn't end up in jail."

I don't think Lisa had thought of that. Or maybe she had, and she figured it couldn't be helped, this was the only way she would escape a place like Albion. She had that side to her. I always sensed she was a girl who would do whatever she needed to do to get what she wanted.

"I'm sure he'll be okay," said Lisa. "He didn't do anything wrong. He's a smart man. They'll believe him."

She sounded like she was trying to convince herself. Maybe she was. Maybe everybody has to convince themselves they didn't do something wrong when they do something all for themselves.

"Lisa?" I said. "When you get back from California, I want you and me to get married. Let's get married, okay?"

It seems strange now that I would have just come out like that and asked. And I've wondered, over the years, if I really meant it, or if I just asked because I was supposed to ask, or if I didn't I knew I'd never get another chance. It was a dumb thing to say. It seemed a dumb thing as soon as I said it, and it seems dumber now.

Lisa Mullins laughed. It wasn't even a real laugh, more like my mom had done when I asked her, that morning, if after last night she thought Mr. Fairchild might become her steady guy. She laughed as if that were a dumb thing, too, and now Lisa Mullins laughed the same way and I could picture her in a gas station phone booth, shaking her head and rolling her blue eyes at the new kid Prather, though of course I didn't know if he was even there. But I pictured it, Lisa moving her pretty face side to side, the fingers of her free hand fiddling with the buttons of her blouse.

"Oh, Chet. Don't be such a creep. I'm done with all that. I'm leaving Albion. I wouldn't marry you if I loved you."

I didn't say anything. There was nothing to say. I hadn't yet found out, although maybe I had but didn't know it, that love doesn't always matter. But that was the first time, which is the same as the last, and I couldn't think of any way to reply.

"Chet, I gotta go. I'm running out of change. Do me a favor, will you?"

"Sure," I said. For I imagine I was still hoping for something from Lisa Mullins, some small sign, a piece of evidence that the world was like I had thought it was, or how it should be, that a girl should keep on meaning something to me if I said I loved her. Or me mean something to her. "Whatever you need."

"Tell Mr. Fairchild goodbye for me. Tell him I'm okay. Tell him I had to go. I had to. He'll understand. Tell him it was time for me to leave Albion, to get away, and that's it. No other reason. It was just time for me to leave. Or I might never have gone."

"You want me to tell him all that?"

"Yeah, all of it. At least as much as you can."

I heard someone say something to Lisa, a voice other than her own. Was it Prather? Or just somebody who wanted to use the phone. I didn't want to hang up.

"Where are you, Lisa? Where are you calling from?"

"Nowhere, Chet. It doesn't matter. Just tell Mr. Fairchild what I told you, okay? You'll do that?"

"Sure," I said, lying. I wasn't going to tell him anything. I knew that and I suppose Lisa Mullins knew it, too. But asking me was part of it. She had to do that much. "I'll tell him everything you said. I'll tell him the whole thing. I'll tell him you said thanks for the flies, too."

There was a brief pause while Lisa tried to figure out what to say. I imagine she even thought about hanging up. But then she'd have me—besides Mr. Fairchild—knowing what kind of girl she really was. And maybe one day Prather. And on and on, until enough guys knew and she *was* that kind of girl whether she liked it or not.

"What are you talking about, Chet? What flies?"

"The flies Mr. Fairchild gave you last night. Ones my mother gave him and then he gave to you. When he saw you last night."

"I didn't see Mr. Fairchild last night," said Lisa Mullins. "I don't know anything about any goddamn flies. What are you talking about, Chet? What's this got to do—"

I hung up. That was the least I could do to make Lisa Mullins be quiet, to stop her from lying anymore. Of course she had to lie, just as I had to lie in telling her I would say goodbye for her to Mr. Fairchild. If she wanted to know more, she'd just have to come back.

She didn't of course, come back that is, not for a long time, not until it didn't matter, the valley had become what it is today. The prison opened that summer and suddenly Albion seemed somehow foreign to me, a place I could no longer understand, as if the trees themselves turned blue, the River Beulah red.

But Prather returned, two days after Lisa called, and though that eventually explained a lot of things—if not the flies my mother gave Mr. Fairchild that ended up on Lisa Mullins' bed—Prather's return did nothing to keep the valley from changing as though the river seen through broken glass.

I don't know what kind of trouble Prather got into when he got back. But it occurred to me at school the next day that he might have an idea about my mother's flies. I said something to her that afternoon, but she just shook her head, casting shadows over her work, and said that wasn't the point anymore.

"You like to tell me what the point is then?" I said.

My mother set down her scissors. She wasn't used to me talking to her like that, but if nothing else this whole episode with Lisa Mullins and Mr. Fairchild—and maybe Prather, too—had shown me you could get away with talk like that, that you didn't always have to keep quiet about how you feel. My mother raised the lamp from above her vise. She twisted toward me atop her stool, the exact same way, I learned later in life, a guy in a bar will turn when he's ready to fight.

"The point, Chet, is your friend Mr. Fairchild is in trouble for teasing that snake Lisa Mullins out of her hole. The flies don't matter, Chet. The Prather kid doesn't matter. What matters is that we put an end to this nonsense and get this valley back to normal."

"And Mr. Fairchild packing?"

"Or a short visit to our new prison. Derrick Prather says he can arrange a bed for Mr. Fairchild anytime soon."

I felt something then, a sensation inside me that would one day signal a fear of what lay ahead. But at that moment it seemed but another of many feelings I noticed without being able to identify.

"I'm sure he can," I said. "Especially if he knows his pissant son got those flies somehow from Mr. Fairchild and made it *look* like Mr. Fairchild is in the wrong."

My mother shook her head. She raised a hand and drew the hair off the side of her face. She kept her bangs short then, so she didn't have to do anything to keep them from falling into her eyes, but she had the habit of running a finger over an ear, as though to remind herself she was still pretty despite doing what some people thought of as man's work. She looked at me as if I were an odd new fly she had just been given to tie.

"You still don't get it, Chet. You miss the point. Lisa Mullins and Prather are kids. They don't know any better. Mr. Fairchild made this happen. He's the adult. He caused it to happen."

"Yeah, he did," I said, turning to leave the room.

So I suspect it was my mother who spoke to Prather's father about my suspicions, and that he told Prather what I thought. All of this seems petty now, small-minded, the kind of intricate details that really don't matter, that just get in the way when people want a feeling of control over what does and doesn't go on. The details can tell the story but they can also get in the way of the truth. Nobody ever once got a fish to talk—but they can sure as hell tell you why fish rise.

The next week at school Prather approached me before classes and said I was talking shit about him. He was wearing his California outfit, nothing different really than what lots of kids wore, only none of it, you felt, had you seen in stores in Albion. We were over near the senior lockers, and I pretty much ignored Prather until he raised his voice so everybody around us could hear.

"And who do you think you are, telling people I took Fairchild's flies to give to Lisa? What kind of crap is that?"

"I told my mother," I said.

"Well that's just about the same thing as telling the whole fucking valley."

Prather looked around, smiling. Now that I think about it, he looked around at the kids who had started to gather about the same way Mr. Fairchild had looked that first day when he told Prather that he should take up fishing. But the kids didn't give him back what they had given Mr. Fairchild. They stood and looked, waiting to see what I would do.

For a moment I didn't know. What Prather said about my mother was true, and I guess I had reached that point in life when a kid is pretty sure his mother—and his dad if he has one—shouldn't be trusted. Not that that means you don't love them. But loving some-body and believing them are two different things, and right then I was as ready to tell my mother to go to hell as I was to say the same to Prather.

"Or is that your way to get Fairchild off the hook so you two lover boys can go fishing again?"

It was all pretty simple after that. I made sure Prather knew the exact spot on the river he could find me any day, after school, he wanted. There's a long run below the turnout just past Second Creek, and for the next two weeks I went there directly from school, driving the little Honda my mother planned to give me that Christmas so that she could get something new. By then there was only an hour or so of light to fish after school, but the first of the winter-runs were in, swimming up with the rains, and I got two that first week waiting for Prather and lost another that bounced twice across the river before coming unbuttoned.

I have to wonder if Prather came by every day, spotting my car, and then decided against hiking down to the river. Maybe he *was* afraid. Maybe he didn't want to let on—even if it was only to him-self—that my hunch was right and he had taken those flies out of Mr. Fairchild's truck and left them lying on Lisa's bed. He was a punk, I can tell you that, a kid with a hotshot dad who thought he could come up here and make this valley his own. No doubt Lisa Mullins gave him reason to think that, too. And by the time he did finally show up on the river, my mom and his dad were doing more than bad-mouthing Mr. Fairchild's naughty ways, which, anyway, sounded more and more each time just like the kind of thing kids said about one another all the time.

But of course what Prather and I fought about that day on the riv-er—a cold day, December by then with the trees dripping even when it wasn't raining, so that you never really knew whether it was rain or not, just this cold mist falling from above—was nothing more than what we could have fought about that first day he looked through the open buttons of Lisa Mullins' plain white blouse. We didn't fight that time because I still believed in something, the possibility that a Lisa Mullins might be something more than someone to desire and love. And that men like Mr. Fairchild were better than they really are. I was just a kid, a punk, too. And so it was that kind of fight, the kind kids have, before you learn what life is really like and how to go about hurting someone the best way you can.

# *six*

# Lake
# Albion

It seems so obvious to him that he hates to even think about it. The same week he starts in after steelhead, he meets a gal who sets his heart racing, consuming his thoughts both on and off the water. She's single, retired, pretty as a model, with property in the upper valley she manages for profits he finds staggering in comparison to his twenty-three-year-career teaching salary. All week he fails to move a fish, hardly remarkable in the middle of August, high bright sun flooding the canyon, the heat and harsh light driving him off the water the same hour the rest of the world heads off to work. He can't figure out what she does all day. He tries phoning as soon as he arrives home, late afternoon, early evening. But all he gets is her voice mail, and not once does she return his call.

It feels like a damn cliché: can't get a fish, can't get a date. At his age, however, he understands the perils of pressing on either front. He's a patient man. You have to be. These things can take time. All of which, repeated absentmindedly as he tugs off his waders, sound to him like more clichés, corporate platitudes, the painful banalities released by even his most precocious students. *Pick up the damn phone*, he says out loud, stepping into his moccasins while he taps in her number on the cordless hung just inside the garage door.

She answers on the first ring. Startled, he recites his entire name, adopting a tone he normally reserves for nosy parents. He tries again—"The fisherman?"—anticipating the question. But it comes out sounding like an answer from a clueless kid called on in class.

"I've been trying to get ahold of you," he adds.

"Well, now you have, Mr. Elliot Merrick. What's up?"

Mocking him? That's fair, he concludes, accustomed to taking the higher ground.

In a short while they've reached an agreement to do something together. At first it's nothing more than that—they'll figure something out. Yet this immediate progress inspires him to liken the call to that inevitable first steelhead of the season: the unexpected grab, his initial clumsy response, the timeless thrill of a big fish taking line, the wail of the whirling reel. Maybe tomorrow. He's due. Pacing as they talk, he returns to the garage and collects his steelhead vest, still wet from a deep, midmorning wade. Fishing? Of course he'd take her fishing. Tomorrow? Tomorrow would be great. In the kitchen he hangs the vest from a chair, removes the fly box and sets it open on the counter for any damp flies to dry. Lake Albion still has plenty of trout, he suggests. He'll bring his canoe. He can give her a casting lesson, and they can spend the whole afternoon—

"I'm busy after lunch," she says.

"Busy?"

"After lunch. I have some things I have to do. We can go first thing in the morning, can't we?"

He slides the fly box into a corner of the counter, flushing the lid with the sharp Formica edges. He usually doesn't get home from fishing, from steelhead fishing, he explains, until late morning, maybe even noon.

"I've got a plumber showing up at an empty rental before noon," she counters, "a building inspector sometime between then and four. They won't get any more specific than that. You know how it is with tax-paid employees," she adds.

He doesn't reply, studying the neat rows of colorful flies, surface patterns on one side of the box, elegant, sparsely dressed wet flies on the other.

"You want a date, Mr. Elliot Merrick, act now or you're back in line."

❧

He picks her up at seven. They ride in bursts of animated exchange up the forested valley, drinking coffee poured black from his Aladdin thermos. At the lake they discover one other car, a pontoon boat moving mercurially in the brilliant early light. Unloading the canoe, he's forced to consider the formal outline of her heart-shaped bottom, displayed in khaki capris against the blue of the quiet water. He puts up rods. One cast demonstrates she has no experience, and he settles into the easy pace of the morning—so unlike steelheading—walking her through the basics of presentation while here and there trout open perfect circles upon the smooth surface of the lake.

The rhythm of the feeding has quickened by the time they climb into the canoe and slip from shore. *Callibaetis.* Yet he refrains from naming the hatch, just as he has resisted all temptations to loose his fly and cover a rise. He would really like this healthy, handsome, independent woman to favor his company, an ambition he balances delicately against the ill will generated by his angling expertise throughout much of his romantic past.

"Shouldn't we be able to catch these fish?" she asks, stabbing the air with the blade of her paddle.

"Absolutely."

He directs her to set down the paddle and ready her rod. Beyond her, feeding fish dimple reflections of basalt scree as if drops of reluctant rain.

"Put your fly in the water and let out some line."

"That's it?"

"For now," he says.

He locates the pontoon boat and selects a course roughly parallel to it and the earthen dam. Sunlight creeps into his shoulders, tight from a week wielding a two-handed rod, and from the cover of his sunglasses he steals glances at her trim ankles and an ageless turn of her calves. Stirred by the rising trout, he resists the urge to satisfy his curiosity about her past. Stories of failed love, he decides, are one and the same, his own included. Paddling slowly, he watches her rod tip, held at an angle that suggests a readiness to deal slicing blows, and he considers why, at the beginning, so many women—but rarely men—command the rod as though gripping the neck of a frightened rodent.

"Should I do anything?"

"Not until you feel something. Then just lift the tip of the rod."

Feeding trout reveal themselves in all directions from the canoe. Above them, swallows swirl like ashes in incomprehensible flight. Something tightens her line. She lets out a yelp, and her excitement rocks the canoe, forcing him to hold perfectly still.

With little coaching she manages to reel in a foot-long rainbow and hoist it aboard. They share an uneasy moment when she asks that they keep the fish to eat. As these are stocked fish, dumped here by the thousands, he agrees, but while the trout flops at their feet, he finds himself without any reasonable means to kill it. These days he doesn't even carry a pocketknife to school, much less while trout fishing. He tries holding the fish in one hand and thumping its skull with flicks of his middle finger, an attempt that proves as feeble as spitting to put out a fire. Embarrassed, he proceeds to lift the trout by its tail, turn it upside down, and whack it, head first, against the canoe's hardwood yoke, dislodging an eye that protrudes accusingly while he strings the fish through the gills from a length of tippet material.

"I hate when people let their fish just suffocate or drown," he intones, dangling the darkening trout into the water.

"We don't have to worry about that one suffering," she says, and the smile she offers seems, from his angle, true as a fool's beneath the color in her sunlit cheeks.

By the time they've reached the middle of the dam, three fish hang from the improvised stringer. He begins casting, surprised to see the pontoon boat, manned by a fellow somewhere near his own age, closing in on them, although he can't be certain if this is by design or the result of their new, drifting course. Falling off from the dam, they gain sight of the mountain, blatant with snow against the flat blue sky. They share exclamations. The air stirs, riffling the lake, the sun honing gradients that will sharpen, he suspects, within the hour, and when the canoe pivots, swinging broadside to the breeze, the pontoon boat lies directly in their path.

"Doing any good?" he calls across the water.

"I am," the fellow answers. "But I'm not killing anything."

For the briefest of moments he tries to imagine that he has heard incorrectly. Then he looks to her for reason not to reply. At the same instant, he recognizes that were she not with him, this rude response would not have occurred.

But that's hardly the point, he concludes.

He glances at the fellow long enough to see that he is dragging a fly through the water, fishing exactly as she is. Later, he will often wonder how much she understood, the pettiness, the insults intended and implied. The sport's history is long, traditions old and, for outsiders, arcane. As a woman she might well have been privy to the currents of his emotions, a notion he will entertain until deciding, later still, that his motives, in this case, were as shallow as a dog's.

He instructs her to exchange rods. She takes his and, as directed, casts toward the pontoon boat. The leader straightens in the breeze. The fly, a bold-profiled parachute Adams he tied to his tippet when he spotted the first *callibaetis* from shore, rides the gentle chop between the boats, its white wingpost visible, he thinks, as a middle finger.

"Cast again," he says, and as she does, he sweeps the canoe forward, within measured range of the high-floating rubber craft.

"Hey," says the fellow, close enough now he needn't raise his voice. "You going to cast right in my fucking lap?"

"Don't worry," he replies, stirring his paddle to stop and steady the canoe. "Can't you tell she's a beginner? She could never hit a target that small."

They all stare silently a moment at the fly on the water. He feels in his heart the trajectory of an anger pure as love. Suddenly a trout appears beneath the fly and in the same instant eats it. Practiced now, she raises the rod, stops the fish and reels in quickly. She lifts the trout from the water, swings it over the gunwale and into his reach. He bats it once with his free hand, sets down his paddle and catches the fish in both hands. Clutching it, he casts glances side to side, bidding his audience to settle his resolve. Then he grins at both of them, raises his eyebrows—and he thrusts the trout in his mouth and bites off its head.

The plumber phones while she fixes trout almondine. At least that's what she's called it, half in jest, blanching all four fish in a cast iron skillet. Oily skin on her hands, she nods toward her cell phone, asks him to read the number displayed.

"He'll figure I got hung up," she says, afterwards, wrapping soiled fingers around the stem of her glass of chardonnay.

Nothing more is said about the ill-treated trout. In the morning he ties on his Waking Muddler, the first time all steelhead season he's felt confident to swing a surface fly. He raises two fish, hooks and lands them both, and in the afternoon he calls to invite her to share the hatchery fish he killed. She doesn't answer. It's a month before she even leaves a message. She's met someone, she says, and she'd rather he not call.

*seven*

# Chernobyl, Idaho

We talked about Idaho for two years. And it became clear this summer that we would end up talking about Idaho again, and doing nothing else to get there, if we waited for the perfect time to go. My oldest son, Speed, had acquired his mother's thirteen-year-old Corolla, tying him to a steady job, and on weekends and days off he liked to drive to the city and hang out with his skateboarding friends. My other son, Patch—who enjoys nothing better than a fishing trip with the three of us together, if only because it means he gets his big brother's attention, good or bad, all to himself—seemed leery of leaving the state, as if asked to engage in a foreign mission that would require unusual or even secret tactics. My own schedule held openings left and right— although you'd be surprised how quickly a teacher's summer calendar fills up, especially if he's given up the pretense, once and for all, that there is anything that matters more in life than fly fishing.

Or maybe it was me doing all of the talking. You can get a lot of mileage out of a phrase like "unsophisticated westslope cutthroat rising freely to oversized dry flies." I took Patch to a tiny neighborhood creek, tangled in the shade of alders, fir, and vine maple, and for the first time he witnessed trout materializing in the perfect clarity of seemingly empty pools, each fish appearing as if by optical deceit, a trick in editing, moments before attacking the fly. The biggest fish approached double digits—that is, it might have gone ten inches. Yet whatever else the claims made for fly fishing—and I'd be the first to admit the claptrap and mumbo jumbo—whatever else the pretext or even apology, nothing accounts for the sport more graphically than sight of a trout launching itself from oblivion to intercept the path of a floating fly.

The fellow at the fly shop in Lewiston, where we pick up licenses for ten days, says fishing is slow. In exchange for the encouragement, and better directions than I have to Kelly Creek, I buy a half-dozen flies, caddis and hopper patterns everybody knows but that I've never gotten around to tying. Outside, July heat, cause of the unfavorable fishing report, swells beneath the curious inversion dynamics that can make Lewiston, in summer, feel like Downey, California, and in winter, between spells of brilliant sunshine, like the underside, says one local, of ice in a frozen dog bowl.

But that is the Clearwater out by the Potlatch mill, and as I aim the van up Highway 12, I try to recall my Trey Combs, what I know about this great river, its oversized B-run steelhead, the rich tradition of surface patterns and the names and personalities of anglers who pioneered this unique, inland, anadromous fishery. And then, more soberly, farther up the road, I take in the Dworshak hatchery, mitigation for Dworshak Dam, the criminal strangulation of the river's North Fork and the demise of its own magnificent steelhead run, so deeply imbedded in Jim Harrison's bleak, surrealistic masterpiece, *A Good Day to Die.*

"Before *I* die," I announce, "I'm going to get a steelhead on this river."

Throughout a bend in the highway I study another broad text-book riffle and perfectly delineated run, imagining the kind of long-distance cast that happens only rarely outside of my imagination, the swing of a sparsely dressed muddler waking seductively in a broad arc etched as crisply as a boat wake into the surface of the wide, blue river.

"I'm sure you will," says Patch, as he does to such assertions of mine, whether he believes them or not.

"You can just see a sixteen-, eighteen-pound fish come up under the fly."

I take my hand off the wheel and make a gesture as if picking an orange off a tree.

"That's a big fish," agrees my son.

But we both know that good fish are never so simple as an act of imagination, and the very best ones seem inevitably to spring from a source as fabulous as the reservoir of our strangest dreams. We follow the river and I suffer the sudden anxiety that so often strikes at the start of a fishing trip to someplace new without benefit of someone along who's been there before. Will we find fish? Will we find the water? I glance over at Patch but he has already descended into one of seventeen library books—from Cormier to Sleator to Paulsen—that speak of his own concerns about this adventure. He knows the magnitude of neglect his father is capable of in the heat of any number of fishing scenarios. I silently grieve my distasteful past, knowing full well I have no intention of changing my ways. The best that can be said for both of us, I think, is that we each believe the other capable of deciding what is best for himself.

"How 'bout some ice cream?" I ask, an hour later, in the last town before we leave pavement and head into the fold of the Bitterroots.

We cross into a new drainage, escaping the smoke-like valley haze. Tangles of blurred wildflowers rush by. A creek appears through the trees, transposing itself with each sweep of the rutted road. I catch my mind wandering, returning to an old dream revisited the previous night, a place that has grown so familiar over the years that I recall it as if I fish there for real. I used to think it was Yellowstone; it's more a region than a specific piece of water, an entire suite of creeks and rivers and pools, riffles and runs and even roads, turnouts, and trails, all of the snippets and snapshots that make up a favorite destination one frequents when one takes to the road.

But this is nowhere. Not only is the location imaginary, I recognize nothing in any of the scenes that comprise the dream from anyplace I've ever fished. Bouncing through the curves, the creek gaining strength by the mile, I find it daunting the mind capable of repeatedly conjuring such persistent, vivid images out of nothing that actually exists. More troubling still is the appearance of late of Patch in these dreams, such that, at times, I feel our experiences together belong to a dimension beyond what we merely do and say, the casts we make and the fish we catch. Yet I convince myself, again, that this is somehow no different than the experience of visiting a new spot with a picture in your mind that turns out completely wrong: The guy said the water is like this, the trees and mountains like that, the fish this and that—but none of it, nothing at all, squares with the reality of the scene now before you.

Current bends around a single, isolated granite boulder with the precision of wood grain colliding with a knot. Patch has found the sweet spot—an almost perfect cylinder of blue-black water that disappears into promising nothingness. He drops his fly, again, on the wrinkled surface, which appears all but static despite tracing the outline of the dark eddy nestled behind the rock. After years of pitching small nymphs into the turmoil of Deschutes River riffles, Patch has only now started to experiment with the necessary adjustments in his cast to ensure his fly lights softly and drifts without drag. From the top of the pool I admire his short stroke and tight, well-formed loop, devoid of bad habits ingrained in my own. I can't see the fly when the small cutthroat pierces the surface of the stream and draws the leader tight into the center of the disturbed water. Rod tip held high, Patch glances my way, perhaps nothing more than the most basic of human reflexes but in my mind a gesture that spells out who he is as much as his sunlit posture and the cut of his jaw.

Our first campsite disappoints us. The campground nearly full, we have to settle for a spot without privacy situated right next to the toilets. Motor homes lumber by, raising dense clouds of parched tal-cummy dust along the adjacent forest service road. The rest of the traffic, both on the road and in the campground, seems made up entirely of four-wheel all-terrain vehicles, or *quads*—although the bark of these ill-bred buggies may account for the imbalanced tally. Slowed by the heat, we allow other anglers in camp to get a jump on us for the evening rise; I have no intention, anyway, of competing for water, as it appears already there is plenty for everyone and happening upon less obvious spots often proves more interesting and just as fruitful as getting first licks on pools you have already fished. Naturally this attitude will change if the fishing turns sour as the ingrate in the Lewiston fly shop predicted. We eat a leisurely early dinner of gourmet hot dogs grilled in a skillet on the Coleman stove— and then something comes over me while I'm telling the story of a thoughtless angler who trashed his own water, destroying the place he loved. "What kind of guy would do that?" I pronounce, and I fling the last of my dinner over my head and into the trees. Patch seems as astonished as he is amused by this impulsive act, although his laughter is genuine and later while we're fishing he repeats the line a number of times so that I can see it will be woven into the fabric of our dialogue. "What kind of guy would do that!" Before climbing into my sleeping bag in the back of the van I step into the darkness next to the bushes rather than walk over to the toilets and then realize, with my fly unbuttoned, that I'm about to pee on our fly rods. Back in the van I explain to Patch what just happened, sparking a fresh burst of laughter that brings to mind the purity of silliness that in families, at least, remains available without drink or drugs.

Looking for bigger fish we head downstream. We follow the well-traveled motor home road, treated in this stretch to prevent dust, along the fork of the river below the creek where we are camped, targeting that imprecise amalgamation of variables that ranks one likely spot above the others. Eventually I settle on a deep shaded run that requires we wade halfway across the river to an island tangled with fallen trees left behind by high water. Patch accepts my hand during the deepest part of the crossing; from the van the clarity of the river had promised deceptively shallow access to the partially hidden run. Once in the shadows I position Patch in line with the best of the obvious holding water. He delivers a large Royal Trude into the current, a cast that sends me scurrying across submerged rocks to likely water of my own.

Returning to camp after morning fishing we find open sites close to the creek, tucked beneath tall firs and pines. I let Patch pick the spot he likes best. He hauls our small wood pile over to the new site while I load our cooking gear into the van and circle the campground and unload again. Deep shade offers respite from the heat although we find ourselves lethargic in the early afternoon, stretched out on our sleeping pads while reading and trying to nap. Patch has already calculated that he needs to read a book and a half a day to work through his stack and he appears to be keeping pace. He's not crazy about some of my selections, a reaction I'm familiar with from teaching, but he seems reluctant to put down a book he has begun. I suggest from my prone position that perhaps the books I chose are "too realistic, concerned with the kind of everyday problems that don't necessarily make for entertaining reading." This remark earns me a complacent shrug, followed by Patch holding up his book and pointing at it, a gesture that means that's all well and fine but right now he'd like to continue reading.

That evening we run into our first spell of challenging fishing: sporadic rises begin to appear on a wide, smooth tailout, but nowhere in the vicinity of our high-floating dries. The pool runs close to both the road and the campground; it must receive steady pressure. These fish are no dummies. I rush through a gamut of flies, wading deeper and deeper until I realize I'm low enough in the tail of the pool to cross. Patch stands in water up to his waist, making long casts that much more difficult, and even his best efforts fail to reach the deepest current, where the rises grow increasingly steady. On the far side of the river I'm able to work my way into a favorable casting position; I finally settle on a small dark soft-hackled diving caddis, which I dead drift in the film on casts directly across the current on a line all but taut. The light falls and I get two good fish and miss several other rises at a point where I can't tell if the fly is starting to swing or if, shortly before it drags, the line is merely influencing the fly, as an old buddy used to say. By the time I cross the tailout again I have to call Patch's name to find him through the darkness. He's still in the river, without a rise, he says later, despite cast after cast and the flurry of feeding trout.

A pattern begins to emerge. I let Patch sleep in each morning while I sit at the fire drinking coffee and reading an oversized Russell Banks novel until an unspecified moment propels me back to the van, where Patch lies burrowed in his sleeping bag on the backseat. We eat a hearty breakfast—pancakes, eggs, bacon or sausage; one of the few skills I've learned over the years when in fishing camps is to eat big but less often, ensuring more time on the water. Patch doesn't share my enthusiasm for this stratagem; he fills his plate once and that's it. He also lacks the stimulation of a quart of coffee. I don't rush him, but I keep him moving. Dishes? Yeah, right.

Late morning, when sunlight falls on the water and the fishing slows, Patch retreats to the bank and takes a book from my pack. Here and there little yellow stoneflies flutter through the air, as graceless as falling leaves; in smooth water I'm able to inspire several impressive rises with a yellow-bodied parachute Adams, a color that means the fly isn't an Adams at all, but that's what I call it anyway, for lack of a better name. Patch comes over with the camera to take photos of the best fish; when I get two more quick fish in a row he puts away his book and brings his rod. I direct him to the band of water through which the best fish have risen with cat-like assurance. He hooks a good fish and I hurry for the camera. I get one grip-and-grin shot, another close-up of the fish, golden and green as if filleted from the mossy granite streambed. While Patch releases the trout I study him through the viewfinder. Is it my imagination or has he adopted a look of detached cool, despite the smile, when gazing back at the camera, the expressionless posturing of a teenager? Or a seasoned angler? Or so unlike his father, beaming goofily back at the inside joke of his self-refracted image? Patch casts briefly without moving from the one spot then reels up his line and heads back to his book. I switch to a partridge and yellow soft hackle and leave him the best water, swinging long casts quartered downstream through a chattering riffle.

Sunday, a travel day. We drive fifty miles to the nearest town, refuel, buy ice, and hurry through a pile each of machine-dispensed ice cream, slumping in the midday heat. We follow three different rivers and end up in a campground that feels just this side of a trailer park: campsites crowded along oblong loops with special attention to the needs of motor homes the length of train cars, plus the requisite vehicle in tow. Wobbly from the heat by the time we trace our route on foot back to the Loop C self-serve pay station, I second-guess our decision to stay. But the guy back home, I explain to Patch, said this is a river we want to fish, and we both agree we've been driving for miles along good water. That evening we get skunked—not just shut out, but along the entirety of what appears a textbook pool, wide and smooth and the color of a dawn sky, we fail to sight a single rise. Nothing. In camp we sit up late poking at the fire while heat lightning flashes beyond the ridge of mountains descending diagonally across the northern sky.

"It's just too hot here," I conclude. "The fish must be higher up."

"They have to be somewhere," offers Patch, sharpening the blackened end of a stick on a rock.

"Leroy Hyatt said they can travel seventy miles. You just have to find them, he said."

"Leroy who?" Patch asks, impaling a marshmallow.

We spend the next morning working our way up river, stopping at likely looking water without finding signs of fish. We pass the last named spot on the map—gas station and store, diner, cabins, a campground—and continue climbing toward a pass, the river growing smaller. I find a narrow turnout and park the van above a tight, shaded pool, twisting between boulders at the base of a riprap embankment. As I pull rods from the back of the van, Patch says he'll stay there and read.

I understand. We've been at this routine for hours; the appeal wanes. I clamber down the rocks, aiming for a spot, brilliant in the sun, from which to pitch a short line across the dark current slipping through the shadow of the ascending forest. The fly falls in the throat of the pool and a trout rises and eats it, exposing a broad flank of speckled green and gold. Immediately the fish is on the reel, taking line, and before I can hold it, it plunges over a small fall into the pool below.

I holler for Patch. Picking my way across the tops of the sharply angled rocks, I holler again for him, and once more when the fish bulls its way into the depths of the new pool, darting first one way and then the other in short bursts of surprising power. The rim of rocks at the edge of the road remains empty. I shout once more for Patch—then decide I need to take care of the business at hand, regardless of whether the act is witnessed by my private audience.

The trout proves bigger than anything we've seen all trip, closer to eighteen than sixteen inches, not a hog but impressive nonetheless, especially in water this size. I return to the first pool and take another good fish, inches shorter than the first but still as thick as the best fish we've caught up until now. I climb the steep rocks to get Patch; he's lying on the back seat, book held high, shielding his eyes from sunlight angling through the window while he reads.

"Found some," I announce, swinging open the back doors of the van. Patch's head rises over the back of the seat. "I shouted up here a couple times," I add.

Patch removes a finger held inside his book. He checks the page number, inserts a scrap of yellow notepad paper as a bookmark.

"I thought I heard something," he says.

We move into the new campground, passed on our way upriver. Only a few spots are taken; we settle into a riverview site, free of neighbors as far as we can see through the trees. Felled timber lies conveniently around the margins. I take a handsaw, cut rounds, and set up Patch with the splitting maul. He swaggers after one particularly accurate hit. Heat prevents us from going very hard. Patch lights a Citronella candle, to ward off bugs, and sets it next to his book and a canvas chair. I wander off to the river.

We have a spot picked out to return to after our early dinner, only to find a car in the turnout, two guys perched atop separate rocks. We head a hundred yards downriver, where we had planned to cross anyway, but in the low light the deepest seams near the broadest reach look dark with possibilities. I've found nothing but six and eight inch fish since the two good fish far upriver; I'm moved to try something new. We're still missing an essential ingredient, I think, something to make this river reveal itself in a different, prophetic way.

I have two Chernobyl Ants that Gary Davis, from Vacaville, sent me, along with other samples of his work, after I took him trout fishing on the Deschutes. I tie on the smaller of the pair. In all my life I've never fished with a floating rubber fly. I flip the beast onto the water and practically laugh as it wobbles by. A few casts later, when the fly disappears, sucked through the surface in a toilet-flush boil, the take seems inevitable as the setting sun.

The following days I fish Chernobyl Ants more and more, switching first to the bigger of the two, then buying a handful of them, big as bath toys, from a display of locally tied flies in the campground store. Never often, but time and again, thick handsome trout slip through the opaque surface of the river, intercepting the course of these goofy flies with abrupt, iridescent finality.

Yet Patch stands back from this sudden fortuitous sport. The clumsy flies are awkward to cast, twisting anything lighter than 3X tippet into an ever-shortening snarl—and Patch proves reluctant to switch from the typical hairwing fly, as if these new rubber monstrosities are the unsavory secret weapon he had feared we need resort to upon venturing this far from home. I know better than to push him. Whatever this is we're doing together seems to hinge on a single shared promise: We're neither of us here to tell the other what to do.

～

Our last morning Patch hardly fishes at all. He says he wants to finish the book he's reading; he adds a second one to my daypack, and somewhere along the water I notice he has finished the first one and started the other. Remarkably, it seems to me in all of this, is the ability on both our parts to remain free of guilt and obligation while choosing to do as we please. Back in camp for our afternoon meal, Patch shushes me a few times when, fueled by food and fresh coffee, I lose myself in retellings of two more remarkable rises to my wriggly rubber flies. He lowers his eyes to his book, the stink of Citronella rising between us.

But late in the afternoon, while I'm climbing into my waders, Patch rises from his chair alongside the trunk of the broadest of mountain hemlocks, approaches me directly, and announces he's ready to fish "from now until dark."

"I was reading about a boy who almost misses his chance," he explains. "I thought, 'We're here in Idaho; who knows when we'll be back.'"

"Misses his chance to do what?" I ask.

"Oh, you know, the usual stuff: Save the world from evil. Make it a better place to live."

Patch offers these modest objectives from the back seat of the van, where he changes into his undergarments before pulling on his waders. I try to catch a look at him while he struggles, unawares, with the twisted straps and irresolute buckles: Is he for real? Save the world? A better place to live? I search his open, unlined face for a trace of guile, some hint that he's pulling my leg, making light of this whole silly adventure we call fly fishing that threatens, again and again, to subsume one if not both of our lives.

But irony, I decide, belongs to a literature that still fails to capture my son. "Save the world?" I all but shout. "What kind of guy would do that!"

Before heading to the water, we paw through the Altoids tin I'm using to hold the big Chernobyl Ants that have suddenly elevated this trip to Like-Never-Before status. Patch chooses, instead, a bullet-headed, rubber-legged, golden McSalmon, one of the other ridiculously oversized dry flies I acquired in that flush of giddy buying while fingering the locally-tied wares. In the course of the evening, I get three more broad-shouldered greenbacks to rise majestically to the ugly rubber bug—while Patch fails to move anything larger than fingerlings, casting determinedly into the waning light. Just before quitting, I wonder if I should have insisted he use the same fly I tied on.

Wading through the dark, I decide it's too late to worry about that now.

# *eight*

# Modest Perversions

Ellery Quayle isn't surprised when she catches her boss, Nathan Beal, listening in the empty hallway outside the open classroom door of the new English teacher, Melissa Day. She would have never suspected her principal of such transgressions. But when she comes upon him, still as a scarecrow above the summer-waxed linoleum, his head tilted forward with the intent concentration of someone boring through a wall with his ears, she feels his behavior in character. Nathan Beal smiles at her without making any move to leave his post. That evening, as she sits with a fist-sized glass of Cotes de Rhone while taking in the sad neglect of her summer annuals, Ellery attempts to conjure a professional spin on this otherwise menacing act, failing to do so even as the wine and fading light soften the autumnal gloom of her withering garden.

In the morning before classes she finds Missy Day in the copy room and relates what she has seen the previous afternoon. Concerned about alarming the new teacher, she presses for a level of ironic detachment that comes out sounding like nervous, seed-eating chatter. She wonders if she she's becoming a "gossipy, premenopausal bitch," a phrase she has heard the three other young women in the English department, all of them married, use to refer to a pair of weathered secretaries in the front office. Missy Day, a handsome, horsy woman who appears to favor midcalf skirts and plain, close-fitting tops that accentuate the thickness she carries through the shoulders and back, removes a stack of pronoun worksheets from the copier and carries them to the paper cutter, where she aligns the pages with crisp jolts along each edge.

"You think he's dangerous?" she asks.

Ellery is quite certain she rarely knows what she thinks anymore. "Power," she remarks, "provides opportunities for abuse." Her tone seems to her more and more these days a form of controlled hysteria. She studies the new teacher's face for any suggestion, however faint, of rolling eyes. She gratefully notes the steady, delphinium-blue of Missy Day's interested gaze.

"The question of danger is one that every woman must inevitably ask," tries Ellery.

She goes right ahead and recounts the brief history of her dating Nathan Beal. She is still troubled by the thought that, for a spell of a few weeks, she believed something would come of these epileptic encounters. Nothing can be further from the truth, she hears herself saying, than an equation balancing sex and love.

"I call them dates because Mr. Beal brought to the table the sophisticated companionship of a teenager. Otherwise I might refer to our time together as evenings spent with a Whoopee cushion."

Harsh, she thinks. She accompanies Missy Day through the lockered halls to the English department, recalling the moment she irrationally proclaimed "That's it!" during a rare bout of robust lovemaking atop an armrest of her reupholstered sofa. The memory embarrasses her. She feels a dapple of warmth, as if the afterglow of a day spent spring gardening, spread beneath her eyes.

"I just wanted to tell you what I saw," says Ellery, bracing open the door with her hip.

"Thank you. I appreciate your concern." Missy Day passes into the room, turning slightly to avoid brushing against Ellery. She lowers herself into a plastic chair in front of one of two computers, her eyes already fixed upon the screen. "I guess I'll be careful what I say."

They begin meeting after school, out beyond the football field and ag building where Ellery maintains a complicated array of targets for girls in her archery club who want to practice during the off-season. It's an excuse for her to shoot as well. Taken by the sport since her two older brothers erected a stack of hay bales behind the long-abandoned chicken house their father, a middle school math teacher, always referred to as a barn, she competed at the college level, helping the small teachers school she attended in eastern Oregon win its first and only NAIA division three championship her senior year. The professed benefits of the sport for budding adolescent girls was not lost on her, either. Yet two decades of concentrated effort have done nothing Ellery can discern to improve her cleavage, although her grip, men have told her, feels unusually strong.

Missy Day proves a willing student. Her powerful upper body produces a statuesque profile as she concentrates on a target, and Ellery is quick to point out the deep penetration her new friend is able to achieve with her arrows, even as her aim shows little in the way of improvement. Both women agree the main purpose of meeting, however, is to venture outdoors to enjoy the mild fall afternoons before time changes at the end of October. Plus, confides Ellery, they will soon be "up to their nostrils" grading papers, an analogy she settled on long ago to describe her struggles with depression and alcohol brought on by responding to the needs of a hundred and fifty students, a frequent sense of feeling overwhelmed that mars her otherwise successful teaching career.

"But I never drink when I'm shooting," Ellery states pointedly, elevating a clear plastic cup of sangria she mixed that morning and then stored in an Aladdin thermos kept overnight in the freezer in anticipation of another ninety-degree afternoon, perhaps the last of the year. She hands the cup to Missy Day. "I couldn't stand the results if I did."

Ellery sips from her own cup, peering over the sharp edge as the young teacher, radiant in sunlight, smiles back at her. She has noticed Missy Day quick to respond to even small amounts of alcohol; she tries to recall a time when, for herself, drinking provided not just relief but actual pleasure. Above Missy Day, Ellery studies the robin-breast tinted pears crowding the limbs of the orchard abutting the high school property. She feels the same distended heaviness of the trees with their ripening fruit, as if her own body is carrying a seasonal load that threatens to break her. She raises her free hand to her open neckline, the flesh there still moist from three-quarters of an hour of serious shooting. She tries to imagine a warm smile on her own face. Discouraged by her mood, she allows her gaze to drift off in the direction of the school—and she watches as Nathan Beal, in Dockers, topsiders, and Hawaiian shirt, approaches purposefully across the straw-colored grass.

"Well, look who's here."

Missy Day turns, spotting the principal. She downs the rest of her drink, looking around for a place to stash her glass.

"Don't bother," says Ellery, emptying her glass nonetheless. "What we do on our time is none of his business."

"We're on school property," offers Missy Day.

"And Nathan Beal doesn't know his ass from a hot rock."

The two women watch as their principal stops at the target they have been using and inspects the cluster of arrows Ellery left stud-

ding the bull's-eye. He removes one of the arrows and runs a thumb
over the rounded silver tip. He holds the arrow up to his face, closes
one eye, and sights down the shaft from behind the yellow and white
plastic fletching. Nathan Beal continues toward them, balancing the
arrow, point down, on his middle finger.

Ellery Quayle and Missy Day look at each other and shake their
heads.

"Ladies."

"Sir?"

"I'd heard you two were up to mischief out here these days.
Thought I'd come see for myself."

"As you can see, it's all true." Ellery places a hand on Missy Day's
bare, sun-tanned shoulder. She is startled by what feels to her as round
and solid as a football. Yet the skin lies soft beneath her fingertips, the
surface warm from the sun. Surprised by the sensations produced by
this casual gesture, Ellery sets her empty cup atop her head and sticks
out her tongue at Nathan Beal. "Care to join us?"

She reaches for the bow left leaning against the chain link fence.

"I really came out here to see if Melissa needs anything. We all
know how tough it is the first year."

Ellery stands with the bow, unstrung, in her outstretched hand
until Nathan Beal has no choice but to take it. He props it upright at
his feet, flexing the fiberglass slightly.

"I take it, Miss Day, Ms. Quayle has provided everything you
need to get off on the right foot?"

Missy Day glances at Ellery and nods. "I'd be lost without her."

"Not surprising. Ms. Quayle is one of our heroes. This school
couldn't get along without her."

Nathan Beal smiles at Ellery. She wonders what it would feel like
to punch him in the nose. She watches with interest as he lifts the
bowstring away from the bow and steps a leg through the opening.
He forces the bow to bend around the back of his thigh until he is

able to slide the top loop of the string into place. He checks to make sure both loops are properly seated. Nathan Beal tugs on the taut string.

"This'll be fun," he says. "Been awhile."

Ellery tries to recall any mention of archery, besides her own, from their incandescent past. All she can think of is that damned exclamation she unwittingly released atop the sofa, plus an occasion when Nathan Beal managed to guide her up onto the Formica kitchen counter for what she commonly referred to in emails to her remaining unmarried classmates from teacher school as "cunning linguistics." Cunning, indeed, she reminds herself, watching Nathan Beal toe the fifteen-yard stripe, a handful of arrows deposited carelessly at his feet.

"We need to go stand behind him," says Ellery. "Safety first."

She leads Missy Day beyond the faintly chalked line. Adjusting his stance, Nathan Beal indulges in the glow of attention Ellery has long recognized as the archer's singular grace. Maybe he will be good at this, too.

"I actually owned a bow when I first moved to the valley." He notches an arrow and allows the bow to hang perpendicularly in front of him. "A cedar longbow. But it soon became apparent the sport here embraced a redneck mentality and nothing more. I was in it more for the personal growth. *Zen and the Art of Archery*. That sort of thing."

"Interesting," says Ellery, barely able to contain the urge to say *right on* or *far out*.

Nathan Beal checks his feet one last time. He raises the bow, draws back the string to the corner of his mouth, and aims. His arms are steady, his posture erect. He releases his shot. The arrow rises steadily above the target and disappears into the pear-laden trees.

"A 'Stadler,'" says Ellery. "We call that a 'Stadler.'"

Missy Day looks to both her principal and her department head for further comment. Nathan Beal stands tugging on the bowstring, as if trying to determine the cause of his errant shot.

"They own that orchard," says Ellery, pointing with a nod and her eyes.

"At least for now," adds Nathan Beal, notching a second arrow.

A week before the annual Stadler Halloween party, to which teachers are encouraged each year by a Nathan Beal email to attend, Ellery discovers via the three married English teachers that Missy Day has "gone out with the boss."

She has seven minutes until class but she exits the English office and presses through the milling students, who part upon her approach as if schooling shad. Outside Missy Day's room Ellery forces herself to stop and breathe. She tries to catch sight of her reflection in the door's narrow glass window, patterned with chicken wire that suddenly reminds her of the wire egg holders she and her brothers used to color Easter eggs in unsuccessful attempts to brighten up their father's chickens' brown eggs. She feels a surge of resentment for a wealth of unspecified pain, the sources for which include herself. Failing to find her face in the glass, she concludes she looks terrible, an assessment that takes less and less imagination these days as she descends into the rhythm of evenings drinking and grading.

"If you fucked him I'll absolutely scream." Ellery slides into a chair affixed by bent chrome tubing to its Bakelite desk. She sets her folded hands before her in what she hopes approaches an attitude of piety or prayer. She feels certain that even if Missy Day and Nathan Beal have "gone all the way," there can't yet be lasting damage.

She throws her hands in the air. "Oh, how *could* you!" she exclaims.

Ellery struggles insensibly with her composure as she watches Missy Day rise smiling from behind the cluttered desk. The young

113

teacher turns to a computer—How'd she get that already?—and clicks the mouse. She has her hair knotted atop her head, exposing her stout, unlined neck and the abrupt sweep of those startlingly broad shoulders—and Ellery tries to recall examples of Sagittarian imagery but can only come up with unrelated mythological deities that, anyway, always look too feminine for warring gods. She wants to believe the very best about Missy Day. But her capacity for such faith dwindles as she takes in each gesture of innocence—the upturned palms, the welded smile, a sudden hefting of the curve of Missy Day's shoulders toward her pretty, unmarked ears.

"We just went out. It was fine."

"So it begins," Ellery laments.

"Not if I don't want it to." Missy Day folds her arms beneath the rise and fall of her perilous bosom. "You act as if this guy is some kind of two-peckered billy goat."

"Those are his words!" cries Ellery, jumping to her feet, banging the tops of both her knees on the edge of the desk. She attempts to glare but feels reduced even further by the effort.

Missy Day stares back at her.

The young teacher lowers her eyes.

"Okay, you're right. And Nate Beal is a sweet guy. How can you not like him?"

"I knew it!" Ellery covers her ears. "Don't say another word!"

All morning while attempting to wrap up her unit on the myth of Minotaur, Ellery feels stricken by Missy Day's sudden impropriety. But it isn't that, she decides at lunch, Triscuits and peanut butter and a Bartlett pear eaten alone in her classroom. Missy Day is twice the— what?—twice the *creature* Nathan Beal is. Missy Day can eat Nathan Beal, a reckless trope that makes Ellery's upper lip quiver with rage.

During her last period prep Ellery returns from the copy room and halts in the hallway just short of the corner beyond which stands the door into Missy Day's classroom. She can tell the door is open;

Missy Day's voice pours into the hallway with a new teacher's resilient belief that it is possible to talk over the swollen, glandular rumblings of a roomful of teenagers. Ellery notes distractedly the persistent, patterned use of the first and second person pronouns ("I need you . . . . I want you . . . . I asked you . . . .")—and then she is aware, as if conscious again of her breathing, of the immediate presence of Nathan Beal. She makes no move to go farther. She is sure he is listening, too—somewhere in the hallway around the corner, just as she saw before. That . . . dog. She feels certain of his presence in the same way she knows, the instant before release, her arrows will find their marks, so certain she resolves not to step forward and catch Nathan Beal again, fearful of the magnitude of self-loathing should she be wrong.

The Robin Hood costume seemed the obvious choice eleven years ago when Ellery received her first invitation, handwritten from Nathan Beal, to attend the Halloween party for school employees staged annually by Frank and Tillie Stadler. The Stadlers offered use of their home as longtime members of the local school board, the closest thing to an illuminati, Ellery soon learned, a valley this size would ever see. Or need. Fresh out of teacher college, Ellery fashioned her costume with intent of drawing attention to her intelligence, wit, the subtleties of her physical charms, plus direct and literary allusions to what she thought of then as her outlaw spirit. Over the years, however, she has modified the costume to where, even though everyone knows she is Robin Hood, what with the bow and all, there remains little that resembles the striking balance of her original design and anybody's recollections of the leader of Nottingham's merry men.

This year's slitted skirt, for instance, serves no purpose but to make as many men as possible, including Nathan Beal, uncomfortable in her presence. Strategically aligned, each aperture affords view of just enough thigh to bring into serious question whether or not any other article of clothing could possibly fit inside. Striding toward the punch bowls, still undecided whether to draw from the one labeled *With* or the one labeled *Without*, Ellery is certain she overhears somebody from a cluster of coaches and social studies teachers state he can "take it or leave it." Lifting from a stack of plastic cups, she accepts the possibility that such statements might also have nothing to do with her. But as she swirls the ladle through the floating pear and apple slices in the punch bowl designated *Without*, she feels a hand touch her shoulder, and she turns and looks into the made-up eyes of Marianne Futar, flanked by the other two young wives of the department, the three of them dressed up as the witches—or, in some texts, three weird sisters—from *Macbeth*.

"Is that belly stud real?" asks Marianne, pointing at Ellery's craftily exposed midriff.

"Real as real," says Ellery, and she sips from her unleavened drink, sensing that without something stronger, this is as close as she will come all evening to voicing a genuine witticism.

"Ellery! Ellery! Come here, my dear! Let me get a better look at that skirt!"

Tillie Stadler waves at her from behind strands of black crepe paper suspended from cabinets above the kitchen sink. Five years ago the Stadlers hired Erik Trammell to remove a wall, leaving the kitchen open to both the dining room and living room beyond—"The last penny we will ever put into this dump," Tillie Stadler claimed. She is dressed, as she is each year, in a pirate outfit, including a black patch over the eye she lost in an orchard accident two years before retiring from the English department—the position Ellery was originally hired to fill. Ellery carries her punch and bow to the tiled bar extending from the back of the kitchen sink and adjacent counters, conscious of the gentle sway of her loaded quiver where the thin strap angles between her breasts, a sensation she wonders if Tillie Stadler, a survivor of two breast-cancer operations, can still enjoy.

"Your house looks terrific," she says, gesturing with an end of the bow.

"Oh, god, no. Anything but." Tillie Stadler runs the back of a thin, sun-weathered forearm over the top of her closely shorn white hair. "This dump is nothing but work."

"Why don't you hire somebody?"

"What's the point? The help seems more work than doing it yourself."

Tillie Stadler dries her splotchy, arthritic hands on a black towel hanging from a belt at her waist. She rests her palms on opposite sides of the sink and leans her failing body Ellery's way. She and Frank, she confides, have all but decided to sell, taking the money they will get from the school district to buy, outright, a brand-new condominium in town. "We could walk to the post office and never have to drive up or down a hill in winter to get to the grocery store or to Wal-Mart."

"What about the orchard?" asks Ellery. "Frank would go crazy without it, wouldn't he?"

"Hardly. All he cares about anymore is his golf and the school football team. He wants nothing from this place or from me."

"Nothing?"

"Not one thing."

These confidences sadden Ellery. There seemed some point once to finding a lifelong partner—but these days she can rarely fabricate an argument that holds water. She stands the bow at her feet, looking down at her silly skirt.

"Anyway," says Tillie, standing up straight. "Nathan has been pressuring us for years to sell so he can build that stadium he's always wanted." She depresses the plunger in a plastic bottle and works lotion into her twisted hands.

"Don't sell because of him," says Ellery. "It's just another schlong thing."

Tillie Stadler rolls her good eye. "*I* know that. But maybe he's right: it might be just what this valley needs." That same eye takes in the crowd that has filled her home. "Where is Nate, anyway?"

Like a lot of people in the valley, Tillie Stadler still thinks of Ellery and the principal as an item—a form of tribal memory that infuriated Ellery for the first year after her break-up with Nathan Beal. Now she feels immune to such modest perversions. She allows her gaze to drift from the crowded room, and she directs her attention toward some vague middle distance that includes the very spot where the arrow shot by Nathan Beal disappeared into the Stadler pear orchard.

"Probably outside pacing off the fifty-yard line."

"Well, he'll be here. You can bet on that." Tillie Stadler turns and lifts a sauce pan of bubbling caramel from the stove. "Love your costume," she adds. "The hat says it all."

Ellery makes her way back to the punch bowl, considering the damage to her already fragile reputation were she to let go and drink herself into submission. She enjoys the ring of the words *shit-faced* as she voices them in her head. What a marvelous language she has dedicated her life to teach!

She is relieved of these private locutions by the arrival of Missy Day, conveniently done up to approximate the tawdry spectacle of a hundred-dollar whore. She will have no trouble eviscerating this floozy should it come to that. She believes it won't. Missy Day has on a skirt that makes her own, vents and all, look like a maternity gown. That skirt, thinks Ellery, belongs around that girl's neck. She feels as sexy as a rock. She can recall no point to being nice.

Missy Day deposits what looks to Ellery like a jacket made from a dead monkey into a simulated casket set along a wall of the Stadler entryway for just this purpose. She parades across the Pergo flooring Frank installed during Tillie's first breast cancer convalescence.

Missy Day's own healthy breasts and broad bare shoulders part the costumed crowd as she directs her steps Ellery's way.

"Puss 'n' Boots?"

Ellery points her bow at Missy Day's leather-shrouded calves.

"I thought I'd give them something to talk about."

Missy Day indicates the remaining faculty with the top of her head.

"Gobble gobble," remarks Ellery.

But her humor is short-lived as she recognizes the smell of sex rising from the plenitudinous woman before her. Missy Day smells like the inside of a pumpkin. Worse, she carries the scent of Nathan Beal on her like a bad rash. Ellery follows the gum line behind her lower teeth with the tip of her tongue. She considers the fabulous opportunities for spreading social justice she has missed out on by failing to join the military. She recalls, quite unwittingly, the little murmurs, porcine in nature, Nathan Beal often made upon achieving his climax.

"I think you and I had better step outside."

Ellery ignores Missy Day's questioning look and places a hand between her shoulders and directs her firmly toward the front door.

Tillie Stadler, crabbing through the crowd with an upraised tray of orange and black candied apples, always a hit, calls out across the room. "You two can't leave!"

"Be right back," answers Ellery, and she pats the specious orb of Missy Day's nearest shoulder. "Female trouble."

"Nathan?" mouths Tillie silently amidst a swirl of pivoting heads.

"Were it so simple," says Ellery to herself, refusing eye contact with anyone but her host.

Outside the fall night air stirs against Ellery's bare thighs. Bright stars profile the eastern ridge of the valley. Missy Day scrambles back into her monkey jacket.

"Where is he?"

Ellery leads them through cars arranged erratically in the gravel drive and out to the edge of the Stadler orchards.

"Protecting our joint reputations." Yard lights reveal enough of Missy Day's face for Ellery to see she isn't joking. "Said he'd wait outside awhile. Didn't want to make things too obvious."

"Oh, Missy," says Ellery. For it occurs to her that Missy Day has, along with the rest of it, been drinking. "Nathan Beal's reputation is cast in stone. And in a place this size"—Ellery sweeps her bow across the sky—"yours is now mud."

"I'm flattered."

Nathan Beal, all in black, steps from the orchard darkness— whether an undertaker or the pimp to complement Missy Day's attire, Ellery can't tell. Yet he manages somehow to still look exactly like a high school principal, an unnerving illusion that alarms Ellery to the point that she moves instinctively to Missy Day's side. She believes Nathan capable of despicable acts. Her own sense of culpability intensifies with indications that this promise of Nathan Beal was what attracted her to him in the first place.

"Robin Hood again?" says Nathan. He grips the lapels of his black suit jacket and rocks his head side to side. "I would have thought Cupid would be more like it. You practically served her up to me on a silver platter."

"What's that supposed to mean?" asks Missy Day.

"It means he's grateful for another pretty piece of ass."

"I'm in love with Ms. Day," says Nathan Beal, reaching for Missy Day's arm. She allows him to take it. "I imagine that feels problematic as I wasn't able to attain such feelings for you."

"'Love means I'd do anything for you,'" quotes Ellery, drawing an arrow from her quiver. "'So *you* should do anything for *me*.'" She inserts the tip of the arrow in her mouth and feigns an act of fellatio.

120

"Passions can make us silly."

"And this is something else?"

Ellery wags the moistened arrow tip at Nathan and Missy Day.

"Entirely," answers the principal.

Nathan Beal, holding the back of Missy Day's upper arm as if it were a pickle jar, spins the new teacher in the direction of the party. Ellery notches the arrow to the string of her bow.

"And where do you two think you're going?"

"Inside." Without turning to look back, Nathan Beal raises his free hand, and he indicates the lighted house as if shooting a basketball. Then he pivots his hand, wrist and all, Ellery's way, and he dismisses her with a backward wave. "Tillie Stadler hinted *she* might have a surprise for me tonight as well."

In a single motion Ellery raises the bow, draws back the string, and aims. She recognizes, without actually seeing, the soft pink flesh at the center of Nathan Beal's palm. She releases the arrow, wondering, as she does, how precisely it will find the center of its target.

"Mmmm," grunts Nathan, freeing Missy Day's arm, and he clutches himself at the wrist.

"My God, Ellery!" Missy Day grabs the arrow. She yanks it out of Nathan Beal's hand. Nathan refuses to let go of himself, even as Missy Day tries forcibly to pull his hands apart, and he continues to make the same little pig noises Ellery recalls from their conflicted lovemaking.

"Bound to happen since day one," she observes.

Late that night, beneath a moon that seems to Ellery more tragic than an empty mailbox, she wanders amongst her targets and sips from a bottle of B&B and indulges in fabulous recriminations. Something had to have polluted the gene pool, for instance, for her parents—two reasonably sane and healthy human beings—to have spawned a monster like herself. It all does come down to sex, she decides, although the fluidity of her thinking brought about by the woody alcohol keeps her from reaching any conclusive reason why this is so. She feels the need to investigate the question but who can she talk about it with? She gazes up at the moon and believes she understands the coyote's need to howl. Yet even this understanding seems to her more of a platitude than an actual truth, a moment of insight that reflects so many others she is unable to hold onto it any longer than the sight of a flying arrow.

In her box in the staff mailroom Monday morning Ellery finds a handwritten note from Nathan Beal telling her to see him before school. She notes, just as she did on receiving his invitation to the Stadler party eleven years before, the heart-shaped "n" he used to finish his first name. She decides emphatically that she has not seen a police vehicle when she passed through the front parking lot on her way to the back entrance of the school. She tries to imagine what it would feel like to get fired.

She finds Nathan Beal in his office, seated at a round conference table on which stands a vase of flowers that look to Ellery like a bundle of exploding crayons. Nathan Beal is writing on a yellow note pad. His left hand, bandaged to the elbow, rests atop the surface of the table as if a toy set momentarily aside.

"Can we speak frankly?" asks Nathan Beal.

Ellery agrees they can; yet in her heart she feels certain frankness remains impossible between ex-lovers of any kind. She reaches for the flowers and adjusts the vase a slight turn side to side.

"A get-well present?" she asks.

Nathan Beal, smiling, nods in the direction of his computer, beside which stands a heart-shaped card signed by Missy Day. Ellery allows her eyes to invade the boundaries of Nathan Beal's pad of paper, recognizing immediately a letter addressed to her principal's new lover. She returns to the feel of the glass beneath the cheery flowers—and as she lifts the vase she considers what other transgressions have been committed to arrive at this profusion of color on this November day.

"We didn't see you at the game Saturday," says Nathan Beal.

There is much that Ellery might have made of that pointed "we." But already it is too late. Vase and flowers shatter upon the carpeted floor.

"This cycle of violence will get you nowhere," states Nathan Beal; yet Ellery notes that he remains seated, the bandaged hand removed to the relative safety beneath the table's edge.

She passes from the principal's office through a shower of horrified stares. She is capable, she believes, of denying everything. Love, as she understands it, will prove her right.

# *nine*

# Bluebacks

Bluebacks, he calls them, a name for sea-run cutthroat all but lost in the Northwest lexicon.

Bluebacks. It's an affectation more than anything else, another in a long list of mannerisms Thomas Novak has adopted over the years, affording him the same glow of pretension he claims in referring to his pair of vintage Garrisons by the cane rod builder's illustrious name. Likewise, his favorite casts have grown increasingly dependent on the nomenclature of single-handed Spey casting, and even his simple soft hackles fall under labels gleaned from the literature of timeless British patterns—because everyone knows, believes Thomas, that it's gauche to even hint at Latin anymore.

All of this name-calling inflicts upon his fellow fly fishers gradations of irony and class. If they have connections whatsoever to traditions in the East, listeners of mention to bluebacks will puzzle over the suggestion to Maine's herring or heritage char. And even if versed in regional lore, they might stumble in confusion over a one-of-a-kind landlocked trout from Crescent Lake, a single, remote fishery on the Olympic peninsula. But for Thomas Novak, the allure of the name arises not only from his studied posturing and a wellspring of folk knowledge, but the allusion, however vague, to blue bloods—the class of angler, at least, he feels his finely crafted fly fishing career has finally positioned him to enter.

Name-dropper, upstart, and self-proscribed angling snob, Thomas Novak emerges in black fleece this August morning from a tarp-covered dome tent in the mist of towering cedars within scent of the sea, convinced he's ever closer to manifesting his fabulous dreams. No doubt, he thinks, making for the bushes, he has a chance today to land a blueback, a fish he's read about, talked about, admired conjecturally but never actually seen. Anything's possible, he reminds himself, once the fly's on the water. As for social climbing, he thinks, his back to the morning breeze, he has, behind him in the tent, Eileen Bishop to thank for his latest rung of achievement, a peal of delight issued from the bottom of her highborn lungs, her timeless yawp inspired with all the precision of a perfectly executed cast.

But there's an edge to Eileen's mood as she digs about the perimeter of Thomas's airbed, searching for items of clothing in the scree of their morning lovemaking. Morning? Try the middle of the day, she thinks, squirreling into her underwear. Still, at any hour, it's much too early, she concludes, to allow semantics to pitch her off center, to upset her breathing, to disturb the temper of this not quite brand-new day.

*No frigging way*, she mews, tugging her bra into place.

Yet all the while she dresses, Eileen can't quite shake the feeling that she's been had. Through the roof vent mesh she makes out the woof and warp of the brown plastic tarp Thomas cast across the tent the night before as they headed for bed—a membrane impervious not only to unexpected rain, as Thomas claimed but, it turns out, to dawn's first light as well. An early riser, with intent to choose her moods come the start of each day, Eileen stirred at the usual hour, beginning with the Kegels she has practiced religiously since her first and only child, the initial phase of a morning routine that includes, to varying degrees, what she calls her 3Ms—movement, meditation, and morning pages—all of it interrupted, today, by the darkest of dawns imaginable and Thomas's emphatic rooting, upending the start of her daily balancing act while leaving her squealing, momentarily, like a startled child.

A ploy? A ruse? Deprived of her morning self-nurturing, Eileen finds herself fumbling with clothing, unable to decide how she wants to present herself today to her not yet familiar lover. She fights a brush through her hair and then paws again through her weekend duffel, quickly establishing she's on a camping and fishing trip, not vacation, and any decisions about what to wear have already, essentially, been made. What bothers her most about the course of the morning, she decides, snapping shut her down vest, is Thomas's shady remark, offered at first nudge, about the darkness of dawns beneath the canopy of the coastal rainforest.

*Blueback country*, he mumbled, already nuzzling. *Makes lingering easy.*

Later, he laughed at this so-called mistake, his own failure to notice the tarp he had spread into place while they headed excitedly, and a little drunkenly, inside.

"And I imagined the forest primeval," he claimed, shaking his mussed head—but by then, she recounts, unnerving herself by degree, she had allowed far more than she intended, a pair of squawks that seemed voiced by somebody she hardly knew. That's it!? That's what? she asks now, aiming herself through the unzipped tent door, the veracity of one Thomas Novak in her sights.

He has coffee made and a fire going by the time Eileen steps from the tent. Without speaking, she veers off through undergrowth in the direction of the campground restroom, whether to use it and tidy up or simply venture off on her own, he isn't sure. Their third weekend date, this marks a first attempt to camp together, and at this point Thomas can't tell if Eileen really likes camping, or if it's just the idea of the outdoors that charms her. Nor has he been able to decide if her claim to be a morning person means she enjoys mornings, or if she just likes to get up early and get things done—very possibly on her own. When the wash water in his big enameled pail atop the grill begins to steam, and Eileen has still failed to return, Thomas finds his sexual bravado waning, the humor of the tarp mistaken for the forest dark fading into doubt.

Is she angry?

He refills his cup from the pot on his Coleman stove. Maybe he was a little presumptuous, he thinks. Maybe he took her by surprise. He stokes the fire with the last hunks of alder from one of the bundles they purchased from the self-serve kiosks along the road to the beach, driving directly into the setting sun after leaving Portland early in the afternoon. Crossing the mouth of the Sol Duc, he considered stopping to fish, but he was just as eager to find a secluded campsite in the park, cook the steak and lobster he had bought from Zupan's, and open a bottle of Argyle, the brut she appears to enjoy just as much as he does. He felt, at times, the entire evening bordered on cliché, but Eileen offered no resistance, and when the fog finally rolled in, covering the stars they'd been able to see above the river through a break in the cedars, she wrapped them both in a blanket, intent on finishing the champagne before the chill of the dew drove them to bed.

Granted, thinks Thomas, rising from the sling of his chair, things did get a little ragged toward the end. Is this what's set her off? He walks to the edge of camp, trying to locate the exact spot where he stepped, late last night, into darkness to pee, only to pitch headlong from the lip of the collapsed bank into the bushes below. That could have ruined the weekend. He studies the height of the fall, the tangle of brush grown up around a pair of tree trunks left behind by some distant flood, and he realizes how lucky he was to climb out unscathed. Eileen heard him stirring about in the branches and leaves, but he doubts she actually saw him disappear over the edge, so black were the shadows cast by the glow of the fire, the glare of the lantern.

Still, she didn't exactly bust up laughing, either, recalls Thomas, when he reported the spirit if not letter of his pratfall. Indeed, he thinks, returning to the fire, debauchery doesn't seem high on Eileen's list of amusements. He takes out his pocket knife and opens another bundle of alder, slicing the nylon rope with a practiced swipe of the small blade. No doubt they have differences, he thinks, and not all of them their differences in age, upbringing, education, class. Is she hung over? Maybe he should start some breakfast. But he knows better, already, than to set food before Eileen Bishop until she says she's ready to eat—a mistake, he suddenly realizes, that might have something to do with why she's disappeared this morning.

Thomas stacks more wood on the fire. He tosses in the nylon rope and watches it squiggle and burn and disappear. The fire pops, a shower of sparks erupting from the new wood. What's the big deal? he asks himself. It's not like they haven't agreed, in principle, to explore the intimacies of a genuine relationship. He recalls their first fit of actual lovemaking, when Eileen, after a dozen dates and six months of emails, initiated the act in surprising fashion. They were headed to Beulah, driving east through the Gorge in Eileen's Range Rover, returning from the annual fundraising auction put on in Portland by Oregon Trout, one of several environmental nonprofits throughout the west between which Eileen divided her time. It was at just such an event they had originally met, Thomas, a sales rep for a half-dozen small manufacturers, showing up under the pretense of keeping tabs on donated rods, reels, and waders. Based out of Bend, Eileen passed frequently through Beulah, where her daughter owned and operated the historic hotel overlooking the Columbia, an enterprise Thomas could barely conceive someone so young having the means to purchase or the expertise to run. Typically, Eileen would take a room at the hotel rather than head for Bend, especially after she and Thomas began dating, staying out late sampling food and music from Portland to The Dalles. He had tried, on occasion, to coax her into spending the night at his place, a modest rental with a view, from the only bedroom, of a sliver of Mount Beulah, an offer Eileen each time emphatically declined—which made it even more of a shock when, having suddenly exited the freeway, Eileen nosed the Range Rover into the margins of a trailhead parking lot and, as she later put it, "jumped his bones."

He was startled—but willing. Yet nothing from even his own often silly adulthood prepared him for the embarrassment he felt when, at the height of their passion, he heard a horn honking and he realized they were being watched, about to be busted, or God knows what. Eileen, however, refused to relent—and it was only in the aftermath of her furious desire that he learned it was her fanny banging against the steering wheel that sent the horn into fevered bleating.

*So what about that?* Thomas asks himself. He studies the flames and sporadic sparks of his morning fire, allowing his uncertainties to ascend toward the rhetorical high ground. A shaft of sunlight filters crosswise through the trees, and behind him he sees the ragged edge of nebulous fog that rolled inland late last night and now seems harried into slow retreat. He closes his eyes, willing himself to attempt to accept the great mysteries in the pantomime of love. He knows if he can only find a blueback or two he can frame the day, the weekend, into a picture of coherency and grace. Eileen likes fish—wild fish. Native fish. She's interested in them. She's positioned her life in service to native anadromous fish and, more important, to the

130

rivers and region in which they swim, investing her considerable talents and immeasurable social clout. He'll find her a blueback, thinks Thomas, allowing the first licks of sun to kindle his easy optimism. He'll find her a fricking blueback—and then they'll both enjoy the day, come what may.

"What's that smell?"

Eyeing the coffee on her way into camp, Eileen sees Thomas's head snap up and realizes he was dozing. She goes to the stove and fills the ceramic mug left standing on the park table beside their wine glasses and utensils from the night before. He must have tidied up. She walks behind him, running a finger along the width of his shoulders, and settles into the chair beside him.

"It's the rope from the firewood," says Thomas.

He gestures at the pile near his feet, his moccasins moist from morning dew, and then he quickly tips forward and straightens the stack, aligning each piece as if setting a table. Eileen senses his tension, a kind of pressing of his lips not quite hidden by his moustache and trimmed beard—but she can't tell if it's a response to his getting caught napping or to her sudden departure from camp.

"Plastic shit," says Thomas, holding up a length of blue nylon rope. He stabs at the coals with a fresh chunk of alder, sparks swirling beneath the pail of wash water, and then he wraps the nylon line into a ball and stuffs it into his pocket. "I probably shouldn't have burned it."

"Something stinks," says Eileen, holding her hands toward the fire.

The heat and good coffee help her maintain her restored balance. She's fine now. A walk along the tidal flats toward the mouth of the river; the time to herself; mist curling through the cedars; the foghorn and faint sound of surf from somewhere in the distance; gulls worrying a pair of blue heron rising from the chaos of flood wood trapped by currents indiscernible in the summer light—all of it brought her back from a place where, on leaving the tent, she was suddenly sure she couldn't face Thomas. Not then. Not at that moment. Not with her own silly bark still ringing in her ears.

"Thanks for not making us run off first thing to the fish."

Eileen stands and steps past Thomas again, touching him once more on the back. From the table she gets the wash basin and comes back to the fire and tips water into it from the pail on the grill. She sets the basin on the bench along the table and adds cold water from a plastic jug. There's a towel and a wash cloth and a bar of soap, arranged as neatly as if they were staying at her daughter's hotel. He's a good guy, thinks Eileen, drawing her hair back and pulling it through a black band she's been wearing on her wrist.

"Takes me awhile sometimes to get going," she says, unsnapping her vest.

"There's plenty of time," says Thomas. "We've got all day."

While she washes, the soap and warm water delicious on her face, Eileen watches Thomas, off to her side, trying not to watch her. He sips his coffee, takes out his pocket knife and acts as if cleaning his nails. She takes off her vest and pulls her Capilene up over her head. Wash cloth in hand, she scrubs up under her arms, around her neck, down her chest and along the top and bottom of her sports bra. Rinsing, she's absolutely certain she'll be fine today.

"Sure wish I knew what that smell is."

"Plastic," repeats Thomas. But when he leans forward, making as if to poke again at the fire, he suddenly leaps to his feet and begins shouting, slapping himself as if a nest of hornets has just exploded inside his fleece.

"Jesusgoddamnmother . . . . !"

After he gets his top off, after he holds it up and reveals to her a melted hole that looks as if the work of a close-range shotgun blast; after Thomas inspects the cluster of perforations in his Capilene

132

undershirt that appear as if made by moths or a careless, drunken smoker; after he studies the constellation of glowing red welts raised along the curve of his diaphragm; after all of this, what bothers Eileen most is how much his knowing tone on speaking the word "plastic" resembled his claim, earlier that morning, that the darkness inside their tent was caused by the depth of the forest—instead of the tarp that he himself had pulled in place the night before.

She understands, now, that he wasn't lying—that his confident assertion then was not a ploy or a hungry ruse, that Thomas had, in fact, believed what he said. Eileen feels sure of that—and this feeling inspires a tiny knot of fear to suddenly take shape inside of her, a fear so sharp she's able to isolate the spot in which it lodges the width of a fist below her navel, a fear so dense she's forced to rest a hip against the park table to keep from losing her balance.

He's honest, thinks Eileen, snapping shut her vest. But whether she can trust him is another matter altogether. If he's capable of mis-reading his own perceptions so dramatically, she thinks, what happens, she wonders, when he interprets the act of love?

Her morning mood derailed, Eileen closes her eyes and breathes carefully in the grip of sunlight hanging from the trees. She hears Thomas rustling through the tent, searching for a new layer to wear. The zipper as he comes out and closes the door brings to mind the wail of a chainsaw rising from deep in the woods.

"Let's go find us some bluebacks," chants Thomas, heading for his truck.

*Bluebacks*, thinks Eileen. *Whoever heard anyone call them that?*

Sunlight puddles on the pavement between dense shadows of forest until suddenly flooding the road at the bridge at the confluence of the Sol Duc and the Bogachiel. The two rivers, low and clear as Wyoming trout streams, exert on Thomas a kind of redemptive promise that he recognizes as his chance to turn the morning around. He had planned to run into Forks, buy Eileen a latte and then fish higher in the drainage, maybe even on the Calawah—but at the stop sign past the bridge at the gas pumps and beach rentals, he pauses a moment, the cab of the pickup drenched in sun, and he considers turning around and pulling into Leyendecker Park and starting in right there above the mouth of the Sol Duc.

It's this moment of indecision, he thinks later, that allowed Eileen the chance to suggest they head out to La Push and visit the beach. Faced with the sting of his campfire branding, Thomas felt powerless to object. By the time they reach the parking lot at the trailhead to Third Beach, he's recovered enough to nurse a silent indignation for this sudden change in plans—yet for now he sees no option but to act agreeable and ride out the rest of the morning.

When they come down out of the trees, however, leaving the slippery trail and last of the earthen stairs behind them, Thomas finds himself moved by the sweep of beach and sunlight resting on the windless water. They scramble across a tangle of driftwood, a nest of logs so large they seem woven by storm and high tide into geological tropes. Out on the sand, they pass a hovel of tents and overnight campers before slipping off their boots, and then they ride the pitch of the beach to the firm footing at water's edge, where they trace the margins of the gentle surf, linking hands as their bare feet dip into the cool sea.

Near the cliffs of the headland, they find a secluded spot tucked behind a pair of bleached logs crossed in an attitude of resting chopsticks. Neither of them has brought a bathing suit. But as the sun climbs and warms the sand around them, they peel off one layer after another, until they're down to underwear that looks no different, they both agree, than anything they might have worn had they foreseen this pleasant outing. Then even this layer gets shed—and when Thomas moves a hand onto Eileen's sunny thigh, they both prove incapable of resisting the effect, Eileen rolling to her hands and knees, aiming her bottom in a manner that lifts her free of the worst of the sand, while suggesting to Thomas courtesies that avert irritations left by the morning fire.

Later, in the afterglow of this unexpected good fortune, he considers again the prospects of his and Eileen's farfetched relationship. Perched atop the pair of beached blond logs, he watches Eileen alternately crouch and rise as she rinses in the lapping shorebreak, her movements abrupt, bird-like, her slender legs, long and taut, shaped by the currents of health and good living or an aspect of high-strung compulsiveness, the likes of which make it all but impossible for her to sit still. He doesn't know quite what to make of her. One minute they seem linked by an exquisite attraction that finds them both helpless with desire; the next Eileen behaves as if the mere act of lying beside him leaves her skittish as a stillwater trout. She certainly doesn't need him for anything but the most rudimentary favors, he thinks, a notion that immediately creates in his mind a series of obstacles as he attempts to muster a sense of genuine self-worth.

She has, it would seem, everything anyone could need—a belief, he understands, that reflects his own petty views of class.

What she doesn't have, he concludes, is a single glimpse at a small trout fresh from the sea, one that moves back and forth between saltwater and freshwater as easily as a coastal breeze. She could buy her first look at a blueback, too, he imagines, leaping from his perch to the sand. But that wouldn't be the same thing at all, he decides—anymore than paying for sex, he suspects, buys you anything anyone would call love.

All the way back to the Sol Duc, where Thomas has promised her "the best sport money can't buy," Eileen struggles with the first dour incriminations of love. What is she going to do with this guy? She has, up until now, felt absolutely certain she could treat this weekend as a lark, another in a long run of dates with nothing more at stake than

135

the feeble thrust of companionship and, perhaps, who might choose to assert command come the inevitable march of desires. Now she can't quite figure out what to think. The scent of sea and pleasure pesters her, clinging to the arrogance of her assumed detachment. This is no way for a woman *half* her age to act, she thinks, absorbing glances from Thomas across the width of the pickup cab, his face leaping in and out of the shadows of the passing forest.

By the time he parks, aligning them in the shade of a single cedar cast across a potholed gravel lot, Eileen has decided to put a stop to their heated posturings. She can find no rational reason for allowing herself to fall in love. She climbs out of the cab and meets Thomas at the tailgate, recalling her silly innocence during the long run-up to her marriage, when every man she dated seemed to offer the possibility of something she both needed and desired. And then? Following the birth of Leanne, a decade of unrelenting sadness that still strikes her as the greatest waste of time in her life. The worst of it, she reminds herself, allowing Thomas to put up a rod for her, was that Stephen, her daughter's father, proved a kind and decent man—which made the pain of ultimately rejecting him further undermine her sense of moral worth.

Even now she finds her behavior reproachful. She has no intention of fishing with Thomas; she knows she needs to make some sort of clear gesture of refusal. Yet in her reluctance to speak her mind, she's already permitted his expectations to overrun her own—proving, again, her capacity for submission and deceit. She should stop him. He's tying on a new tippet, for Christ's sake. And yet she recognizes, as well, the pleasure she feels on the receiving end of this kind of service, the attention of a practiced hand—even a bumbling fool like one Thomas Novak. She can't quite help herself—which, in the end, she thinks, has always been her downfall, this lifelong habit of embracing the patronage of those who aim to please her.

136

Adrift in thought, Eileen finds herself at the edge of the lot gazing down into the final rapids of the Sol Duc, pitched in furious descent into a broad, tranquil bend of the Bogachiel. Standing still, she imagines patterns in the rush of the river reverberating against the underpinnings of the new bridge, the fresh slabs of concrete standing in riprap as if stranded above the low yet steepened flows of summer. Her sudden, unconscious retreat from Thomas and his truck strikes her as an act of dissociation. Is this the start of something that happens with age? The knot of fear she has carried all morning in the pit of her stomach bursts into a flood of dread, seeping into her bowels. She reaches out a hand to steady herself against nothing that's there.

Or is it, she asks herself, love?

Eileen closes her eyes, listening to her breathing over the sound of the river. She refuses to entertain notions of genuine romance. Since the end of her marriage two decades ago she has tried, on occasion, to allow herself to descend into the illusion of love. But at all times she feels removed from the actual feeling—as though, she's come to believe, she lacks the imagination to lose herself in the part.

What's important, she tells herself, are these rivers right here in front of her nose—these and a thousand others just like them throughout the West. And the fish that need them, journeying back and forth to the sea. Yet in the midst of her convoluted self-analysis, she manages to fabricate a connection between her own readiness to submit to the attention of others and the long history of environmental degradation throughout the West—as if, somehow, her failures in love reflect the very same forces by which men—yes, men—have ruthlessly extracted all they could from Western rivers as a means to their own ends, the satisfaction of their selfish desires, their vanity, greed, and bombast. Who's got time for love, she thinks—a thought that bears but a moment's scrutiny as she considers, against her grave intestinal stirrings, her futile attempts to effect any meaningful change whatsoever in the precipitous decline of anadromous fisheries along the reach of the eastern Pacific.

"You 'bout ready?"

Despite the swift chatter of the river, Thomas finds it easy wading across basalt shallows exposed by the August flows. He suspects more water would improve his chances—or at least invite more fish into the river, providing cover somewhere beyond the sweep of obvious holding water wedded to the far bank. The skeletal remains, gray and jointed, of a grounded deciduous tree lie choking the throat of the run, and as he approaches, Thomas can't help but picture the sequence of careful casts he'll make through the twisted currents swirling along the flanks and shortened limbs.

He's almost glad that Eileen has chosen not to join him. At first her sudden decision to stay back at the truck while he fished had not only caught him by surprise, but also infuriated him. He felt offended after going to such lengths to bring her here. Yet when he set her rod on the hood of the pickup, leaving it there in case she changed her mind, he realized at least now he could fish in earnest, without jeopardizing his claims on her affections.

Whatever else might or might not be going on between them, it didn't seem to hinge on whether he guided Eileen into fish—blueback, cutthroat, or . . . . speckle-breasted snapper. *The hell with her*, thinks Thomas, suddenly weary of the restraint he's shown for the promise and sake of love.

Well, maybe not restraint, he concedes, retracing the flare-ups of passion that have marked their course, it seems, from the moment he pitched the tent on the peninsula.

And what's any of this got to do with love?

Yet when the fish comes up and eats his fly, swilling it pretty as an oil painting, the first thing Thomas does is look toward the bridge in hopes of seeing Eileen there. Of course she's not, he chides himself, pressuring the fish to keep it away from the hidden limbs of the half-submerged tree. He holds the fish in the pull of the eddy formed where the tree ends, leaning against the bend of the cane—until he's afraid his wayward glance might have already cost him, he's been wrapped around something he can't see.

Then the fish is moving, line whining off the reel, until, in the air, a blister of silver appears as if suspended from the green wall of forest and Thomas eases back a step, gauging how far he can get downstream should it come to that.

It doesn't. Still, by the time he has the fish under control, he's waded downstream enough that when he glances again at the bridge, hoping but not expecting to see Eileen there, he's looking upward instead of across the water, so that it occurs to him—for not the first time in his life—that he's performing for a woman who he feels is above him, for a woman he's elevated, placed on a pedestal to which an invitation rests on his antics or tireless energy or complete immolation of pride. Either that, thinks Thomas, easing the trout through the current, or get her to descend to his level, where, it seems to him, she'll never feel entirely comfortable, no matter what delights she might experience or he might provide.

Or maybe it's his capacity for self-pity, he thinks, that marks the real difference between him and Eileen Bishop.

But the trout is beautiful, bright as polished metal, with a peppering of black spots that suggest the counterintuitive camouflaging of zebra stripes, the perforations of a mysterious ancient script. He turns it over in his hands, recognizing the species' telltale orange slashes at the gills.

*Blueback, my ass*, he thinks. *It's a goddamn miracle.*

Releasing the trout, Thomas is startled by two short blasts from a horn that seems aimed directly at his head. Above him, the silhouette of Eileen's hand, held against the sky, waves at him from the far side of the cab of his pickup.

"It was such a perfect specimen," says Eileen, explaining to Thomas, back in the parking lot, how she spotted him landing the cutthroat as she started across the bridge. She doesn't give him a chance to ask where she was headed in the first place.

"I thought, *Sea-run cutthroat*. I thought, *Blueback*. I thought, *That's a beautiful fish—and that's a beautiful fly fisherman*."

Thomas can't quite figure out this sudden effusive praise. Either Eileen is in fact just a simple fish lover—or something's made her as moody as the summer weather along this rain forest coast. Either way, he doesn't dare say anything that might derail her affection, aimed at him with the surprising force of the sea-run cutthroat recently on his line.

"You could catch one, too," he says, suggesting, with a hand on her shoulder, that the opportunity might not always be theirs. "Where's your rod?"

Eileen turns towards Thomas and looks at him blankly.

"I left it on the truck," he adds.

For a moment, Eileen's gaze reminds Thomas of the cold illegible stare of the trout he just landed.

"Then it must be around here someplace," she says. "You saw as far as I got."

Thomas feels certain, however, that the little five-weight Garrison would have slipped from the hood as soon as the truck started to move—and it's this certainty that allows him to escape the surprise of discovering the remains of that pretty rod lying splintered beneath his truck.

He feels, instead, the air rush out of him—just as it had the night before when he stepped in darkness off the edge of the bank that wasn't there.

Eileen moves close to him and rests a hand across his shoulders.

"You can always buy a new one," she says.

Still in his waders, Thomas kneels in the gravel and reaches for the pieces of the rod one at a time.

"Can't you?" asks Eileen.

# *ten*

# Family
# Matters

My sons and I just got back from a tough few days on Wolf River. Not only was the fishing stingy, nothing close to what I had enjoyed there last year, but the heat was oppressive, the bugs tenacious, our camp site rocky as quarry midden. A guy driving by one morning stopped on the road above and hollered down to inform us that we had pitched our tent in a restricted area, site of flash floods that "arrive without warning, a wall of water—a thousand cfs—from out of the blue." That evening I heard a rumbling that seemed a plausible like-ness of this sort of spontaneous discharge, despite the starry twilight, a distant rolling clatter that finally began to fade just as I spotted a cloud of orange dust rising from the base of the canyon wall, along which ran the road back to town. Could we get out? A night later, all three of us were awakened simultaneously by a violent clanging outside the tent, as if pots and pans wielded by a dissatisfied spouse. Eventually, I recalled the trap I'd set in the engine well of the van, defense against a pack rat like the one that had taken up residence there the year before, severing wires to the fuel pump, leaving me stranded beneath a pretty stand of cottonwoods at river's edge.

In other words, business as usual chasing trout in the West. With one exception: My sons didn't catch fish. I'm loath to report such egregious failure. Neither one. Not a single trout. It seems an impossible spell of futility, a dereliction of duty, and I feel personally responsible, at fault both as a father in charge of his offspring's angling education and as guiding spirit who drags companions to godforsaken places and then fails to get them into fish.

I wish I were a bigger man, capable of absorbing the broader view. Fly fishing can be tough. Experience teaches us to understand the exactitudes of error, the inadequacies of our faulty ways. The complacent angler accepts defeat. The serious practitioner—or the fabulist, at least—acknowledges failure as opportunity to improve, facing the challenge so to avoid further humiliation, disappointment, and grave uncertainties regarding his own moral character.

Fly fishing, anyway, is about more than catching fish.

Isn't it?

On the long drive home I settle on a ringing indictment of self: I haven't taught my sons how to fish. Instead, they know how to cast, tie knots, read water, wade. They know the difference between a stonefly and a caddisfly, a dry fly, a soft hackle, and a nymph. They even know how to cradle fish when posing for the camera. But they still don't know how to *fish*.

Or if they do know, they don't fish on their own—which amounts, essentially, to the same thing as not knowing how.

It's that simple, I decide, gazing through the bug-splattered windshield, the miles unraveling through fields of mown hay woven into the sweep of the interstate: My sons don't fish on their own. They fish with me. They go when I go; they go where I go; they fish with the flies I fish with; they try to catch the exact same fish that I'm fishing for. I'm reminded, sadly, of couples I've known over the years in which one of the partners (usually—but not always—the woman, if I may be so frank) tags along without any genuine interest beyond spending time with the other person. There's nothing wrong with that, of course; relationships inevitably demand we expand our horizons in the name of something bigger than ourselves. But if that's all it is—going along to be with another—then fishing becomes less about sport, art, or a fascination with the natural world and more about duty—the last thing that compels anyone to get better at anything.

There's a reason, I conclude, that these same partnered, go-along individuals will almost always end up putting away their rods at some juncture, leaving the fishing—and all it requires—to the person in the relationship who cared about the sport in the first place. They quit for lack of love. Not love they stopped feeling for the person they started fishing with (although that can happen, believe me); not love they didn't get back in return. No, the love they lack is a love for the fishing itself, that mysterious, visceral attraction which, like all matters of the heart, manifests itself as a willingness to venture into the nether-reaches of ecstasy, obsession, insanity, and shame.

The question, I end up asking myself, chewing on the subject each mile closer to home, is do my sons love to fish? Speed, the oldest, I'm pretty sure doesn't. Not yet. At nineteen, he's intent on creating his own world—soccer, skateboards, hip-hop, and all—not replicating his father's. Patch, however, might be a different story. Sure, at fourteen, he has far less choice in the matter of whether or not he goes fishing. But it has occurred to me, of late, that fly fishing has taken on new dimensions in his life, that it has become part of his identity, wrapped up, perhaps, with his budding cosmology, his world view, and that he may in fact be doomed to love the sport like I do.

I decide, yet again, to pay more attention. He is, after all, my son.

⌒

We start calling it the .22 Hole. Bouncing at the bottom of the canyon, two thousand feet below where we left the van, the river itself offers surprises around every basalt outcropping and tangle of riparian hardwoods and coniferous old growth—fir, larch, spruce, Ponderosa pine. And this particular run features the fly fisher's textbook riffle, bend, and pool, with current rushing across freestones and sweeping through the constricted throat before spreading like firelight through the heart of the hole. In addition, a fallen tree, a sweeper, extends from the far bank, lying parallel to the surface of the pool, its branches, tipped with still-green needles, slipping in and out of the current as if fingers through unkempt hair.

But it is the .22 Hole because of the gun. Holstered and clean, the revolver lay innocently on the broad stretch of pale, silty cobblestone, exposed by the falling flows of summer. Oddly, within a quarter-mile upstream of the gun, I had already found, in the water, a fully outfitted vest, complete with fly boxes, lures, hooks, and jars of bait—plus, in another location, a plastic tackle box so heavy with spinners, plugs, and spoons that I left it resting on a boulder midstream. All of this, mind you, on a wilderness river without any sort of vehicle access closer than that 2,000-foot descent within its entire drainage.

The .22, however, hadn't been in the water; the leather holster and belt looked as though they were fresh off a glass shelf. I picked up the lot and set it out of obvious sight alongside a length of tree trunk lying on the rocks. Whoever it belonged to, I figured, would search enough to find it.

"That wasn't smart to touch the handle," said Patch. "What if someone used that to murder somebody?"

I considered the possibility—and the son of mine who had just suggested it.

"Where do you get this stuff? It's not like we own a TV."

Still, it becomes the .22 Hole—although not so much because of the gun itself, but because it turns out to be a run as elegant as it looks, drawing us back each evening, and we need to call it something. We raise fish to big hairwing dries throughout the pool. But the best trout inevitably come from the ribbon of current directly under the fallen tree, sometimes even after you have drifted the fly through the sweet spot a dozen different times, growing more and more certain there isn't yet another fish willing to rise.

Or after I have. For Patch fails to move one of those good fish from beneath the fallen tree. We end up taking turns on the .22 Hole, and while Patch fishes, I stand alongside him, talking about casting angles, straight and curved leaders, the hidden demons of drag. But the last evening I decide to step back and let him fish on his own. I take a seat on the log next to where I placed the holstered revolver, which, later the first evening, was claimed—rightfully, I believe—from a couple of revelers camped in a nearby meadow. Patch works his way up the run, reaching out with tights loops, closing in on the fallen tree—and it occurs to me, with pleasure, that he wants one of those good fish, and that he is demonstrating an intensity I haven't often seen before.

There's a pretty rise to Patch's fly and he lifts his rod and connects. I come over to watch the action, Patch nimbly moving in and out of the water as the good trout takes out rod-length chunks of line. In a short while the trout is in the shallows, exhausting itself with sharp lunges and sudden twists of its colorful body. Patch guides the fish toward his feet. Then the hook pulls free.

Patch is as startled as I am. But there's something else—a gesture of disappointment, even despair, that runs through Patch's body as clearly as if he has just been touched by fire. He's bummed. In such moments of my own, I'm prone to verbal theatrics and self-effacing histrionics, reactions that I can no longer separate from true feelings and a perverse sense of irony regarding my emotional investment in this silly game. But for Patch this is something new.

I step close and take hold of the leader and inspect the fly. The hook is sharp, although the gap appears slightly narrowed, as if the fly has struck something on a fallen backcast. Maybe. I use my pliers to relieve the bend of the hook, and then I blow the water out of the big Humpy's heavy hackle and wings and hand the fly to Patch.

"You know where they are," I say, gesturing with my head in the direction of the fallen tree. "Now you know the drift they want, too."

Patch wades back into the stream. The next fish, near dusk, ends up where we both can admire it a moment before sending it on its way.

Another canyon. This one I heard about for over ten years, but without the requisite name or location to find and fish it. A friend had been sworn to secrecy by the old-timer who took him there originally. Said friend had faithfully honored his vow, an act of integrity that seems all but saintly in this age of kiss and tell.

But secrets in fly fishing grow fewer each year, and I eventually heard about the canyon from another source, the owner of a new fly shop a half-hour from home. These guys aim to please. *Big* browns, he said. Pocket water. 1X, 0X tippets.

"You gotta stop 'em or else they'll get in the current and spool you."

"Sounds like a place I might've heard of," I said.

I phoned my buddy and asked him if I named the spot, would he tell me I'm right. He said he would. I named it.

"I'm busted," he said.

Patch and I stumble around the top end of the canyon the first evening, spotting dark fish that remind me of basketballs, even though they're far bigger than anything Shaq could palm, wet or dry. Only later do we decide these are carp, coffee-colored behemoths that hang at the edges of boulder-lined, blue-black pools and stir the imagination if not one's sporting appetites. Has my buddy and all of the fly fishing fraternity joined in a decade-long prank, a practical joke, a hoax—just because some guy turned me, Francis Sepic, into a smart-ass protagonist for a novel that pissed off, at one point or another, most every reader, even my immediate family? My paranoia notwithstanding, Patch hooks one of these fish, and by the time I hurry upstream to inspect his efforts, he says he's just about got it whipped.

"I don't think so," I counter, and I rush off further upstream, where I've left my daypack and camera.

When I finally return, Patch stands fiddling with a limp line.

"Hook pulled free," he says.

"I'm sure they're carp," I conclude, still wondering how fly fishers from ten different western states might have managed to play this joke on me. "You probably snagged it."

"They're big whatever they are," allows my son.

In the morning we work our way down the canyon, stopping in pull-outs along the highway and choosing only those stretches of river that look remotely like traditional trout water. That includes about three stops; the rest of the river twists and plummets, rushes and glides, slips and throbs frothy as spilt beer through a steep unstable gorge choked with loose boulders the size of ice chests, furniture, major appliances, SUVs—and garages large enough to house them.

Temperatures climb steeply toward triple digits; the day seems poised already to thwart any attempts to crawl down into the heavy pocket water, where, I suspect, the big trout we're after—if they exist—reside.

149

We wade into a broad straight stretch of river directly below the mouth of the canyon. I throw a long line and a little Olive Bugger, my concession to ignorance on new waters. Patch, far downstream near the van, flips his fly along the edges, an approach that seems to me to mean he's killing time until I figure out something better. Then I hear his voice, and I see him poised, rod tip bent, in an attitude of graceful concentration that seems far beyond his fourteen years.

"I really want to land this," Patch says when I reach him.

"Pick a place to beach it," I offer nervously. "Get it out of the current."

The fish is a trout all right, an immaculate honey-colored brown festooned with bold spots the shade of darkest cherries. Finally, Patch guides it into a little eddy, grass-edged, and he gathers the fish in his hands.

"Big," I observe.

"Size is measured in increments of fear," agrees Patch, quoting the literature.

I take a couple of pictures before Patch revives the trout and releases it. I ask him what he caught it on.

"Woolly Bugger," he says. "One of those ones I tied."

He holds up the fly to show me. Wet and chewed on, it doesn't look much different than when it was new, a year and a half ago when Patch asked me to show him how to tie something for a demonstration speech he had to give at school. He practiced his speech by tying up a half-dozen black Buggers—the only flies he's ever tied.

"That's something," I say. "Your first fish on a fly you tied."

"It is," agrees my son.

"You could be ruined for life."

༄

We find ourselves, later, on one of those trophy-trout tailwaters ballyhooed in the sporting press as must-fish destinations for the modern, kick-ass fly fisher. Every word written about the place turns out to be true. The trout come in three sizes: big, bigger, and biggest. The largest make you wonder why you haven't brought along your steelhead rod. Of course, I can only estimate the actual dimensions of these biggest fish: Hooked on a #22 Midge, they will usually show themselves once or twice, leaving the water by forces that seem to pull rather than push them skyward, a demonstration of ungovernable ballistics that inevitably spells disaster—or at least a painful uncoupling—as the tiny hook peels free from the flesh of these mighty trout.

Patch keeps his distance. There's a madness to fishing for big trout, a tone that began to reverberate back in the sheer, boulder-strewn canyon when we finally decided to plunge into its shadowy maw armed with heavy tippets and Stone Nymphs the breadth of spark plugs. Carp were nowhere to be seen. Instead, brown trout the size of hunting boots slid out of shallow lies tucked in and around the heavy stonework, mouthing the big nymphs as if dogs cued by Tootsie Rolls. I landed some of these fish—certainly no more than half that I touched—while Patch couldn't quite get it right, intimidated, it seemed, by the harsh surroundings, the unstable footing, the heavy water, the big trout that appeared more angry than fearful when hooked, the oversized nymphs and crude casts it took to fish them.

Or maybe it's me acting a little crazy. Every day at the trophy tailwater I say I'm not going to spend four or five straight hours hooking big fish directly below the dam, and every day I end up wading into the empty slot a little earlier in the afternoon, until at night my eyes, blasted by sun and wind—despite high-end optics—feel as if they are coated in sand, a sensation accompanied by steady tears and, each morning, a crust of grit I rake out of my lashes with the tips of my fingers.

"Don't let me start today before four," I say to Patch, peering over the lip of my bowl of yoghurt and granola, having already headed downstream, while Patch slept in, to work a four-inch Vanilla Bugger through a hundred yards of heavy riffles.

"Okay," says Patch, without conviction.

He joins me each evening after the wind has dropped, after the sun has settled toward the horizon, after he's spotted me, from camp, wrestling with a fish or two. There's a big back eddy alongside the spillwater beneath the dam, and instead of wading out into it, where the heavy current advances and recedes with surf-like rhythms, Patch stands back on rocks at the foot of the dam, pitching his midge or emerging mayfly pattern into the complex currents swirling behind me. Several times he hooks big fish in water I've stomped back and forth through while fighting fish of my own. But each time, three evenings in a row, he comes up empty-handed, breaking off a couple of fish, coming unbuttoned on the others, and each loss, I notice, inspires a slightly stronger physical reaction from him, a sharp, sudden gesture of anger, disappointment, disgust, a jerk of the rod, one arm thrust downward, his head snapping forward, his slender shoulders drooping.

I recognize, in other words, that Patch has fallen into one of those archetypal streaks that anglers, if not all of us, suffer—when it seems that fate itself is conspiring against you. And then I ask myself: Is this that thing called love? I've been wondering, I tell myself, if my sons—either of them—will come to love fly fishing. But maybe this is all that love really is: wanting something so badly that it hurts if it gets away. And still wanting it so badly that you're willing to risk the pain of loss again and again.

Patch gets his trophy the last night. Or at least it's a fish to end his streak of bad luck, failure, call it what you will. We both suffer fits of extended anxiety as the big trout sprints and lunges against the hold of the tiny midge—and then the fish is finally in the shallows, its nose on the bank, and Patch is on his knees, his hands quiet on the exhausted trout. We don't have quite enough light for a picture, but

I go ahead and shoot a couple anyway, slowing the shutter speed to 1/15 of a second, a setting at which, I tell Patch, I can't possibly hold the camera steady enough for a clear photo.

"Good enough for a memory," says Patch, lowering the trout to the water, where he revives it scrupulously.

"Nice fish," I say, watching it vanish. I shake Patch's hand.

"*That* was satisfying," he says.

On the long drive west, we pass within striking distance of Wolf River, still a full half-day from home. Midafternoon, I suggest we stop: head upriver, pitch the tent, dice up some Wranglers in a pot of rice pilaf, get a shot at the evening hatch. Patch is all for it.

"Maybe a little redemption," he says.

I turn and look at my son, hidden in the passenger seat behind sunglasses in the glare pouring through the dust-smeared windshield. And for a moment I imagine the two of us riding the lip of that improbable "wall of water"—a thousand cfs from out of the blue—as life pitches us both into the mysteries ahead.

"Redemption?" I finally ask.

"Yeah. I didn't catch a single fish there last time."

"Redemption?" I repeat. "What the hell kind of word is that?"

# eleven

# All Over
# the Map

It's the cherries, Erica claims, each time she tells the story, that set
her off, the sight of them first thing in the morning in the oily light
of the low-ceilinged kitchen, a glazed, peach-colored bowl of purple
Bings on the butcher-block table behind Leonora, the kitchen help,
stirring a vast puddle of chorizo and eggs spattering on a skillet next
to a stack of tortillas as tall as the waiting breakfast plates.

They made her think of home. Home as a place, of course, the
old diminished orchards still hanging on here and there throughout
the Beulah valley, proud remnants of a way of life, she reminds listeners, that launched the trajectory of her remarkable, unforeseen life.
But home, also, as an idea or ideal, the kind of home she had always
believed in until now, where the story begins, when she had suddenly
ceased to nurture the fiction or fantasy of home, had instead rejected
the very thing she had tried for years to create and now she no longer possessed, not anymore, not figuratively nor literally, not after
this, what she had done to escape the fabulous illusion of home and

perhaps even hope itself that she had fabricated in the face of her fears of the unknown.

They seemed impossible, the cherries, as incongruous as her own presence in the close pungent kitchen, the smell of the ocean mixed with the smoky musk of chilies and grease and a kind of white scent of salsa—onions and tomatoes and garlic and lime—that permeated the air as if condensate of the frying Mexican food. Cherries in the tropics? And even today, retelling the story, Erica Barrett remembers how it struck her then that she didn't know if she were actually in the tropics, if this part of Baja were in fact that far south, and how this improbable appearance of the fruit of her childhood good fortune below a trivial stripe of geography seemed suddenly to matter if she was going to possibly explain—if only to herself—what she was doing here at this moment in her life.

"¿Como los *cherries* llegan aquí?" she asked, resting a hand on the lip of the bowl.

"'*Cherries*'?"

Leonora, dark and inscrutable as the fruit itself, turned and looked at her, the blade of the spatula ringing in somber rhythms.

"Cherries," Erica repeated, turning the bowl as Leonora's head had turned, just that much—and she realized how silly it was, or awful, that she had never heard the fruit called anything but cherries, that in the rough Spanish she had learned from the pickers in her family's modest orchard, it was always cherries this and cherries that—and nobody she knew as a girl, long ago, in Beulah, had referred to the cherries in any other way.

"*Cerezas*." Leonora gestured with her head, a nod toward the bowl—or perhaps her way of showing respect while addressing the *gringa* guest. "We call '*cerezas*'. My husband. He brings them tonight from La Paz."

Or maybe it was the mention of husbands, Erica suggests, now, when telling it, that, along with the mound of wine-dark cherries in the bowl, set her mind spinning in the direction of the unfathomable mystery of the future, the place she had refused to look at, to peer into, on deciding to pull anchor in the midst of a storm of passion that left her, the first morning, on this new and remote shore. She felt, inside of her, yet another wave of an emotion she was still incapable of naming lift her into a kind of accelerating flight, a sensation she recognized as both frightening and exciting as she was pitched, out of control, into a headlong tumble that both delighted and alarmed her. Just like that. Suddenly—far too suddenly, she believed, for nothing in her life had prepared her for any of this—suddenly she found herself experiencing this sensation again and again, this loss of control, and it was as if, in her mind, she were under the influence of some sort of strange and wonderful drug that had turned her reckless and utterly free.

What, in God's name, had gotten into her?

"¿*Esposo*?" she said. And then, recalls Erica, aware that Leonora's English was at least as good as her own old orchard Spanish, she had allowed herself the easy and habitual gringo retreat into English, an assertion, she recognizes this time, of class and status that went far beyond anything to do with her reckless mood and the assumption, of those who pay, to address the help however they damn well please.

"You're married?"

She startled even herself. For it seemed, even then, a kind of insult or threat or challenge, a reaction, she suspects, to her sudden disregard for her own marriage and abandoned husband. Perhaps, she thinks, it was the abrupt switch to English that gave cause to her failure to note the tone of the question so badly. You're married? It sounded insensitive, patronizing, condescending—her bitter memory of which grew all the more troubling when she pictured the look Leonora gave her, a look that said, I am a woman, of course I'm married—a look that Erica immediately connected to the bowl of

157

cherries in the dark kitchen and the hidden life of this young wife whom she had heard arrive, accompanied by barking dogs, some-time in the middle of the warm Baja night.

She had been awake, sleepless for what seemed like hours next to a man she'd known only two weeks, with whom she had forsaken a husband who, despite his flaws, his mistakes, might still have loved her in some strange, confused way—a love that had grown unbearable in the face of all that life could offer. Startled, humbled, unnerved by a silly bowl of cherries, shaken by her own lack of control from one moment to the next and moved, because of all this, to sudden tears, Erica stepped close to Leonora and, in a gesture of perfect despair, she lifted a heavy platter to receive breakfast for her and her lover and a half-dozen other men with whom her immediate future appeared inextricably linked.

Outside, voices rose with the first hints of daylight outlining the movements of unsettled palms.

Leonora, seeing Erica's tears, asked politely what was wrong.

"Nothing," said Erica, moving a hand from beneath the platter to wipe her eyes.

But there was something wrong, and though uncertain what exactly it might be, she offered Leonora a glimpse, something gen-uine, so that, if nothing else, she confronted the feeling that she'd grown callous and cold, the kind of woman no other woman can trust.

"I'm just a little sad, I guess."

Erica recalls her own weak smile as she gazed into the blackness of Leonora's eyes.

"*Triste,*" she added. "*Tristeza. Tristón. Tristezita*"—falling into the childish orchard talk spoken by pickers young and old, brown and white.

"*¿Tu esposo?*"

Leonora aimed the spatula, not unkindly, in the direction of approaching voices.

"That's not my husband," said Erica. "We're only friends."

She glanced again at the cherries. Then she shrugged her shoulders, a gesture she could still read, retelling it, as one of abject submission to both her situation and the opinion of the only person, besides herself, who seemed, right then, to matter.

"We just came here to go fishing together."

"Fishing?"

Leonora lifted the stack of plates from the tile counter next to the stove.

"Fly fishing. *Con las moscas. Las plumas.*"

Erica made a casting motion with her right hand, even then thinking about the big rods and heavy heads she worried might overwhelm her.

"Fishing?" asked Leonora again. Still holding the stack of plates, she reached with her free arm and took the platter of food balanced in Erica's left hand.

Free of even that one small last responsibility, Erica felt as if gravity itself had ceased to hold onto her—and in a fit of release as pure as her most profound response to the act of love itself, she gave herself over to tears, abandoning herself to the simple question of what in the world she was doing here in the first place.

Even when she tells it now, she asks herself what it is she wanted. What did she expect? What is it she imagined happening when she suddenly and irrevocably took flight?

The short answer to these and the rest of the questions posed, rhetorically, to an audience of one or many, is that she finally just quit. She grew weary of a marriage that came saddled with the price of submission and sequestering, a role that left her heart bereft and numb while her husband, Bo, created a life for himself that kept her close but never in the way.

Bo—short for Bodacious, most everyone believed, from the name of their guide service, "Bodacious Fly Fishing," although the truth is he was Bob, Bob Cox, Robert to his parents and Rob and Robbie and Bobbie and finally Bob, depending on who knew him when and where. He seemed from day one, she always puts it, like a good idea—until one day he didn't. But by then it was too late, they were married, and they stayed married because that was the promise even after they both knew they never stood a chance, not really, not in the long run, not after starting out, right at the beginning, by falling in love with the idea of love, not the real-life flesh-and-blood person who soon enough failed to resemble even a crude approximation of that original, misguided idea.

Bo was the first to go, the one to break the promise, although Erica always claims it could have just as easily been her. Maybe privilege and male entitlement made it less problematic for him. She isn't sure. Bo Cox was a fishing guide like she was a housewife. A trust-funder from Boston, he ran an outfit of hand-to-mouth guides, a pack of trout and steelhead bums that swelled and contracted with the seasons. Mostly, Bo seemed to enjoy purchasing expensive equipment—wooden driftboats, machined alloy reels, classic cane and high-end double-handed rods—while knowing precisely as possible where and when and with what flies to fish, and savoring the taste and sedative effects of medicinal marijuana and single-malt Scotch.

Bo wasn't sick. But most of his guides appeared to suffer from nebulous afflictions that made it virtually impossible for them to get through a day without burning a blunt or firing up a bowl. Given the attention of sympathetic physicians, Oregon law protected them. Bo liked to joke that Oregon guides had high standards, and he always claimed that at least the pot kept his guys from getting real about chasing skirt.

Which was a pretty good dodge once he stumbled onto some new hem of his own and started coming home played out as a big trout ready for release.

Troubled already by Bo's growing disregard for most any activity that included the two of them, Erica marshaled her grievances into a silent campaign against all provisions made, early on, for just this sort of call for forgiveness. Mostly, she had come to resent Bo's persistent refusals to allow her to work side-by-side with him on the water. She could row. She had kayaked up and down the Beulah since grade school, and her father had put her on the sticks of his beater Willys as soon as he saw how much attention she was going to get if she stayed in town while, in fall, caught up in the orchard, he fished the Deschutes for steelhead. Of course all of that rowing, discovered Erica, turned out in the long run to earn her even more attention, her tan the tone of the ears of her family's mongrel Brittany no matter how much sunscreen she applied, and her shoulders and arms and young breasts as sculpted as the clean hard sweep of the wild fish her father loved so much right up to the end. That came sooner than anybody expected, and it had a lot to do, felt Erica, with why Bo could claim her fishing skills weren't what they needed to be for a first-string guide. Every trip her father promised he'd spend more time with her after he got a fish or two—but each steelhead took up so much time, energy, and concentration, that he never did much more than leave Erica back at the boat with a trout rod and box of flies.

Then the bitch got him—the Beulah Bitch kids called it, the cancer, in all different forms, that attacked parents and grandparents in the valley at a rate they argued, even boasted, was higher than elsewhere. Nobody had any real proof, nothing more than anecdotal evidence aimed at the longstanding use of pesticides in the orchards, that swelled each year with a kind of furious crescendo of sweet fruit and sweaty toil that left everyone, workers and land owners alike, dizzy with the flush of profits, real or imagined when penciled out across the reach of the unsparing calendar.

Was this also part of her cause for leaving, asks Erica, this lifetime of bounty and want, of excess and inevitable need that left her always uncertain of how much she really had, mistrustful of the notion there was plenty to go around—incapable, perhaps, of understanding the very concept, however fanciful, of home? Things came and went. And even as a teenager, she reminds listeners, the orchards themselves had already begun to vanish, the one immutable component of her childhood suddenly transformed, here and there, into a final crop of brick, siding, and asphalt-shingled roofs.

There were reasons, anyway, for her sudden flight, some better than others—although Erica is never more emphatic than when she contends she would have never left Bo had he not fallen into his own audacious brand of infidelity, a fabulous, rich-kid's disregard for common courtesy, she thought of it then, that offered him impunity in the face of petty derelictions from closing time until the first cock crowed.

Eventually she followed suit. She wasn't looking so much as she suddenly felt available. To what she wasn't sure. But when she found herself one evening on the dance floor of the New Albion Bar & Grill in the arms of a seasonal guide from Fort Collins, a rangeland eco-system grad student hoping before classes started to find his first steelhead en route to Portland to catch a flight to Baja for a week of bluewater *panga* fishing, she allowed the growing fantasy of escape to consume her as readily as a heat stirred up by her own doing. Nothing in her life had ever made more sense to her. She gave Curtis Lathrop a week of slow dances, tips to elegant holding water, her own hungry mouth and absolutely nothing more—and when he begged her to let him buy her a ticket and pay for a spot on a hosted trip out of Punta Arenas, it was as though she fell under the spell of her own fervent imagination, giving herself over to the act of love with an intensity she hadn't experienced in years.

Reckless? Crazy? Perhaps even cruel? It was all of that, she explains, narrating her own story with a kind of fierce detachment from the harsh image she invariably paints of herself. *Pride invalidates the first-person hero*, Erica often says, and she remains careful to cast herself in an unforgiving light. The invitation came and she took it, vanishing with little more than the clothes on her back. Even her kind old mother, alone in the family house while the orchard was run by the Galvezes, the children, all married, of Ruben Galvez, the Barrett's orchard foreman for ten years preceding her father's death—even her mother was left to wonder where Erica ran off to, an act of selfishness Erica still finds unpardonable. But of course mothers are so often part of the problem for girls and young women, she adds, making a face as if someone had suddenly shined a light in her eyes.

∾

Not until the big van had left the pavement, and was making for the beach through an insult of potholes, washboard, and wallowy stretches of sand, did Erica realize that the driver, Luciano, was Leonora's husband.

She rode directly behind him, shaken by the bad road from a sweaty half-sleep she had fallen into as soon as the tires touched the narrow highway leading south, the first trace of daylight showing above the horizon through the window beside her. Now, against the glass, the tangle of bundled rods shimmied this way and that, and she rested a moist forearm atop them, trying to keep the tips from creeping beyond the back of the driver's seat where, in broken English, Luciano defended his driving skills—and thus his manhood and capacities as Leonora's husband—against the amicable ridicule directed at him from all corners of the van.

163

Most of the men appeared to know him. Beside her, in contrast, Curtis seemed out of place, polite and serious, sweating in silence, unwilling to speak bad Spanish, a Rocky Mountain interloper still planning for a future that couldn't possibly contain the brand of citizenship exhibited by this gaggle of middle-aged West Coast sportsmen. As a group they all voiced squandered opportunities and dreams and past connections to the surf and now appeared, by the looks of things, but one step away from skin cancer, twelve-step programs, and a kind of moral destitution for which the only cure was the humiliation they received by force of big fish that should never be hooked, they all agreed, and fought on fly rods. Erica immediately liked them, the bombast and carnal banter, the complete disregard for any concerns outside of the angling ahead. Climbing into the stuffy van, leading the way because she was the only woman in the group, she had calculated with a kind of giddy repulsion the money tied up in the heavy, oversized reels, let alone the rods, enough to support a family of orchard workers year-round before her father died—and in a moment she still finds auspicious, as soon as she settled onto her end of the cushioned seat and Curtis, beside her, placed a hand high above the hem of her shorts, she spontaneously trapped it beneath her own hand before closing her eyes and sinking, through the heat, into the dizzy crescendo of voices of the other men claiming spots for the ride.

She immediately liked Luciano, too. He reminded her of the oldest Galvez boy, Efren, a smiling, confident kid, secure in his good looks and steady income, a soccer player whom coaches allowed to miss practice for work and with whom Erica had attended middle and high school and even dated—or at least ridden with to town when Efren, on turning sixteen, immediately bought a car, a honey-colored Monte Carlo with spoke rims and tinted windows and a sound system she could feel through the passenger seat and seemed forceful enough to shake the apples and pears still on the trees when the school year began. Eyes closed, Curtis's over-warm hand pressed firmly to her thigh, the van lurching into motion while she held onto the look she had just received of Luciano's open, friendly face, Erica remembered kissing Efren in his car that fall, and how he tasted of salt and the flavors of food she loved more than her mother's own cooking and smelled of something shiny he put in his hair and the smoke of woodstoves and smudge pots and the fire in the fifty-gallon drum that seemed to burn perpetually, night and day, spring and fall, within the compound of pickers' shacks alongside the family orchard—and how the intent of Efren's knowing hands, so different than the grabby thrusts of other boys she had kissed, promised something she wasn't near ready for, yet had made her certain she was headed in that precise direction.

A pale, cloudless sky hovered above the horizon at the edge of the sea when the van, hazy inside with dust and a faint suggestion of air-conditioning, finally came to rest. Ahead, the beach was filled with *pangas* and pickup trucks and men trudging back and forth across the sand carrying bundled rods and reels, ice chests, fuel tanks and day packs and, clearly, the excitement and anticipation shared by fishermen anywhere headed for the water. Erica allowed Luciano to take her hand as he helped his passengers down from the van; his face, dark as a pit, opened up to her against the vast empty sky. And it seemed only fitting she claims, telling it each time, that she and Curtis were assigned to Luciano's boat that first day, that Luciano wasn't just Leonora's husband, not just helping out as a driver, but one of the captains, a *pangero*, a brother and a cousin and a nephew and even an in-law or *cuñado* in a family from Aqua Amarga that had discovered the thrill and financial rewards of guiding fly fishers into the wealth of game that swam within range of bait, and a day's worth of fuel, practically every month of the year.

Fitting, claims Erica, because without this coincidence, or act of fate, or the simple blind movements of the heart, she has no story

165

whatsoever to tell—and for the rest of her life, she contends, she might have remained a girl posing as a woman, much as the men she had always attached herself to came to seem, at last, no better, or worse, than boys she had known for a lifetime.

∾

She likes to speculate when she began to imagine making love with—or even seducing—Luciano.

Was it following the first fish she caught, a skipjack tuna the size and precise configuration of a football, a fish she found shocking it could be so small after fighting it for so long until, finally, Luciano grabbed her leader and, laughing at her shouts and struggle, lifted the fish out of the water at the exact moment her arms felt as though they had gone completely dead?

Or was it later, while watching him fillet the yellowfin tuna she landed, his sun-darkened fingers drawing apart the meat the color of pink grapefruit along the course of the crude knife that sliced through the green and yellow skin as if opening a piece of exotic fruit? Or moments afterward, when the flesh was fashioned into bite-sized chunks atop a plastic cutting board and festooned, from a squeeze tube, with dollops of wasabi the color of kiwi flesh and he offered her the food in a manner that reminded her of Father Rodriguez, the priest who helped serve Communion with Father Paul on Christmas and Easter at St. Mary's, the only times each year her parents made her brave the crowds of Mexicans squeezed tight into the pews? Or when, recoiling against the pungent attack of her own first bite, she watched Luciano serve himself, his puppy-pink tongue darting out to receive the fish and instantly she ceased to recall any visits she had made to any church and why?

Or was it, finally, when she stood for a picture with Luciano, side by side behind a bull dorado spread like a great outstretched wing before them, a fish that had rushed to her fly as if a swath of flame propelled by a gust of wind and then, when hooked, climbed into the air as though tethered to a kite before suddenly racing off in a series of twisting jumps that transformed into one long ceaseless sprint that threatened to empty her reel? Curtis, of course, took the photo—and when she looked at herself and Luciano in the LCD monitor, the two of them smiling like delighted children, their arms all but entwined as they steadied the gaffed and dying fish, she pictured his hand secretly holding hers somewhere behind the wide green flank even though she couldn't recreate the moment in her mind to ascertain if this were anywhere near true.

Or was it nothing like this at all? For always, at the end of these speculations, Erica likes to add that perhaps what started began before she even saw Luciano, that, instead, her sudden desire for him came to life from a seed in her subconscious planted by the bowl of cherries in Leonora's kitchen, a seed long dormant from the fruit of that first kiss that flowered between her and Efren Galvez when she risked her reputation, and her parents' disapproval, on a ride with a picker into town.

Yet, really, she's just as quick to counter, can you imagine her state of mind that day—having just run away from home; catering, for days now, to the wishes of a man she clearly had no future with; alone, practically, in a place she had no connection with, yet that seemed, at times, familiar, as if a place in a dream that one returns to and comes to know but isn't anywhere outside the fabulous absurdities of sleep?

For they embarrass her, too, these speculations, reminding her that hers were the fantasies of a grown-up girl, or the silly make-believe snortings of Bo and his half-cocked guides and, in many cases, the paunchy gray-haired men who shadowed her that week in a masquerade of desire, a kind of habitual posturing of these fun yet oddly sad and sometimes fearful men, any one of whom would have gladly taken her to bed even though most of them lacked the

167

energy to try in earnest after a day on the water fighting fish that had already tested, and occasionally surpassed, the limits of their aging strengths.

∾

Curtis proved plenty strong, physically, and persistent—at times insufferably so. Yet that first evening after fishing he left her on her own. Younger by half than the other men, very near the same age as Luciano, he joined the group at the big dining table on the open patio beneath a *palapa*-style palm-frond roof, trying to insinuate himself into the camaraderie fueled by beer and tequila, the fitful production of elegant flies tied amidst growing clutter at vises positioned around the table, and louder and louder claims of successes and failures on the separate *pangas* that day, all the while waves of Mexican music oompahed from a pair of salt-corroded speakers crackling atop the polished wood bar.

Erica showered and did her best to cover up in enough clothing to deflect attention without drowning her in her own sweat. She didn't want to look like she felt she was going to behave. Brushing her hair, lightened already, it seemed, by a single day in saltwater and tropical sun, she stood balanced on the cool clay floor tiles studying herself in a delaminating bathroom mirror, the weight of her intentions riding low in her stomach, a place she had long associated with illness and fear. Finally, she thought, she understood all that she could expect out of life, and that if there was anything to the notion of being the same as men, it was in a capacity for cruelty that she would have never before thought herself capable of.

She went to the kitchen and helped Leonora fix dinner—beans, rice, the fillets of her dorado breaded and fried in a scrim of oil pungent with garlic, an immense bowl of *ceviche*, chunks of sierra mackerel cooked cold in the fragrant juice of five dozen cherry tomato-sized limes. *Women's work*, thought Erica, mocking herself and the very act that seemed to steady her as she anticipated the spirit of her crime. Luciano, she learned, would be around all week; he'd brought the cherries last night as a "returning home gift," Leonora called it, from La Paz, where he worked at a hotel for mainland tourists as a driver and tour guide and sometimes bartender when the *El Ranchero*—where they were now—wasn't booked with angling guests.

"You're not afraid he's gone so much?" asked Erica, setting down the knife she was using to quarter tomatoes for the *ceviche*. She rested her hands alongside the deep bowl, allowing herself to lean into the edge of the butcher-block table so that it pressed against the precise spot she carried the gravity of her ill-conceived plans.

"Afraid of what?"

Leonora came over and, from the bowl, tasted a piece of fish.

"Afraid of . . . of"—Erica stopped short, unable to find the right words in either Spanish or English. Afraid of what? she asked herself, coming upright, almost balanced, her weight supported gently beneath the palms of her hands. Beside her, Leonora gave off the scent of perfume, stronger than any other smell in the kitchen. "Afraid of him not coming home," she said finally.

Leonora went to the open cupboards and returned with a quart-sized bottle of hot sauce. She upended it and shook out splashes that colored the white fish red.

"My husband wants home also," she said—and for a moment Erica wondered if it was broken English she had heard or something much more profound—a question she didn't answer until she noticed Leonora looking sadly at her, as if she, Erica, would know these things if she weren't a marriage-aged woman fishing with flies, with feathers, far away from home with a man who was only a friend.

Which is all it took, explains Erica, to halt her in her tracks.

Just like that, she says, she realized she was all over the map.

⚬

The men found her the next morning alone on the beach, curled up beneath a bath towel, an empty Don Julio bottle, stubby and squat, tucked with her hands between her thighs. To most of them, her appearance there seemed perfectly normal: She got drunk and passed out. By the looks of her boyfriend, he had done much the same, coming to rest elsewhere in the wake of something he had started during the cocktail fly-tying session the afternoon before. They helped Erica to her feet, got Leonora to help her tidy up and get something in her stomach and ready to fish, and when they took charge of her again, guiding her into the van, they directed her into the front seat so she could suffer alone without the fawnings of her dilettante boyfriend during the half-hour drive to the *panga* site at the southern tip of the bay.

During the ride Luciano looked at her, she imagined, as if she were diseased.

Yet when she found herself free of the van, moving across the sand toward the *pangas* lined up along the edge of the water, like great stitches in the seam between sea and land, she experienced a sense of release that lifted her mood out of the physical ache that gripped her body. Today she was nobody's anything—not a wife, lover, girlfriend, daughter, woman—maybe not even good enough to be anyone's friend. Maybe nothing she did today would matter—at least not to anyone but herself.

Maybe she'd burned every bridge.

Maybe she'd thrown away the goddamn map.

The wind, too, had changed, swinging from the south around the point instead of blowing, as it had the morning before, down the channel alongside Isla Cerralvo. Out toward the lighthouse, sets of waves stood up and dumped directly on the beach, leaving behind cascades of foam that rushed from the crest of the steep berm while out in the trough, just beyond the shorebreak, pelicans pitched them-selves headlong into the water, looking altogether like the carcasses of filleted fish hurled from somewhere far above.

It was the pelicans that nagged at everyone's attention—until, starting where they hit the water, their heavy bills piercing the blue-green surface of the sea, it was as though they had opened a wound that bled like a swiftly growing bruise that filled the water with a shadow spreading to the margins of sight.

"Roosters!" Erica heard someone shout—and she was running before she knew it, sprinting to keep up with or get ahead of, she wasn't sure which, a tangle of men all about her, the weight of the rod in her swinging hand tugging her forward.

The fish numbered in hundreds, perhaps thousands, yet they moved in one great cloud of energy, surging this way and that, erupt-ing in displays of violence that seemed as impractical and elegant as the shorebreak hurling itself upon the beach. Clusters of fish broke from the school and charged the surf then splintered into groups of three fish or four, each fish as long as a man. Overtaking the surf, fish tipped forward and accelerated while bait exploded from the faces of the steepening waves and suddenly the black and silver combs of feeding roosterfish came to life, ignited by the heat of the chase.

Erica plunged in up to her knees. A cast? She felt the possibility of the moment in the same spot she had carried her reckless intent to brave Luciano. You can't just keep saying yes—can you?

Her loop was steady as it rushed from the tip of the stout ten-weight. For a moment, the fly seemed to hang in the middle distance, somewhere beyond the end of the line, before finally falling to the water. The take, immediate and vicious, horrified her. A fish as big as—she is?—just ate her fly.

For a brief instant she felt she still had some semblance of control over what was happening. Or what was about to happen. Her tippet, having survived the awful grab, must be strong enough, she thought, to stop a boat—an image that was swallowed by the sound of the reel as the fish began to abuse the drag.

The heat of the spool against her naked palm did nothing to slow the fish. What now? She watched the backing knot vault from the end of the rod. A wave broke, driving her backward, and she struggled for balance against the pull of the wash rushing around her legs. By now she had an audience, guys and guides, the *pangeros*, hovering about her like crows worrying remains along a busy state highway— and then, suddenly, it seemed to Erica that the scene grew still, that despite the energy and excitement and running fish and racing line and reel, it was just one thing happening all at once, an accumulation of forces acting upon an infinite number of moving parts, all of it part of a whole, no different, she argues now, than the restless imbalance of geology.

She likes most to recall the moment she knelt with the fish for a photo at the edge of the surf. Curtis gave his camera to Luciano; he wanted to join her in the picture. But she steered him away, keeping the fish—and the moment—to herself.

Behind the camera, Luciano offered back to her no trace of emotion, and it seems now to Erica that this attitude of perfect detachment was a result of his life with Leonora and its precise articulation of home. Finally, she says, she understood what home meant—a feeling of safety, absolute safety, whether with someone or alone. Yet each time she tells it, she can never quite recall the full sense revealed to her that moment before the camera, lifting the heavy fish before letting it slide free into the surf—and so she feels compelled to tell it again and again, trying each time to recapture a truth she fears may prove irrecoverably lost.

# twelve

# The Longing
# Pleased

It's the forty-three emails in forty-three days that alert Paddy Francis to his troubled state of mind. The symmetry seems impeccable, yet as he turns from his computer and faces his fly-tying bench, he's quick to note that he might well have claimed the same degree of order yesterday or the day before that. At what point has this run of unanswered emails, sent daily to Emily Thatcher, his standing flame, crossed into the realm of semantics, leaving behind the less rarefied air of a spell of pronounced silence? And what difference might day forty-four make? Or fifty-four? Or a thousand and four? Why forty-three? Paddy Francis asks himself—the kind of question he immediately recognizes as further indication of his anxiety and fitful longing.

His bench is a mess—tools, containers, spools of thread and floss, discarded feathers and dubbing furs, random hooks sprinkled like commas in even the best essays he read while still a high school English teacher—the whole nine yards. The sight depresses him. Yet

173

he has no interest in tidying up, nor desire to work in such confusion. Forty-three days. The counting he understands. Now a fishing guide ten months out of the year, he diligently collects data, paying unflinching attention to numbers of fish hooked, landed, and lost, rejecting the offhanded imprecision of so many of his competitors. What, exactly, he'll ask, is a pretty good day? And at what point does good become hot, hot sick, sick epic? These vague delineations can infuriate him, spurring him to make his own tallies as faultless as possible. How easy it is to claim a twenty-fish day rather than actually record that many fish brought to hand—a line of logic he's been known to employ to achieve a kind of self-righteous probity when he suffers the inevitable poor day of guiding.

Forty-three days without a single response. From the back of the bench he takes up a picture frame, smaller than a credit card, and holds it beneath his tying lamp. He removes the reading glasses hanging from his vise and, pausing, inspects the lenses in the light for dust and grime. Even magnified, the faces in the photo seem as small as trout flies, a comparison he feels might be inaccurate until he finds, in an open box on the cluttered bench, a #18 Blue-Winged Olive Soft-Hackle that completely obscures Emily's hair, her eyes, her smile. But both faces, hers and his, look so thoughtlessly content that they offer nothing new or useful to him—and the two of them, standing no taller than the length of a midsize steelhead hook, remind him somehow of a pair of stoneflies against the pale, nondescript backdrop of an insignificant sweep of the Zumwalt Prairie.

"It's trying to snow."

Paddy returns the tiny picture to the back of the bench as Norine Korda, one of his housemates, pulls off her fleece headband and sets his mail on the counter that separates the kitchen of his basement studio from the rest of his living space. Norine and her husband, Fritz, own the house; they both teach at the high school where Paddy taught until, forestalling a midlife crisis, he retired after twenty years and took up full-time guiding. He glances out the window above his computer, a narrow swath of daylight that offers, when skies are clear, a glimpse of Mt. Beulah to the north.

"Still no word from Emily?"

Norine raps the edge of her own mail on the countertop, straightening the pile as if having just collected a weak show of homework.

Paddy doesn't reply. Beneath the clouds, the frayed hem of an opaque sky, he can see the precise line of snow along the forested hillsides across the Columbia.

"What d'you think it means?" he asks.

"Means she's not available right now. What else can it mean?"

Paddy notes the impatience in his old friend's voice. He turns toward her and rises from his chair.

"Do I just keep waiting?"

"That's one option." Norine stands still as Paddy steps past her and collects his mail. "It's not like you have any other. Unless you want to start looking around again," she adds.

Paddy watches Norine cross the room. A health teacher, she's dressed in sweats and sneakers and a knitted scarf for the fifteen-minute walk home from school. She goes directly to the tying bench and picks up the faux pewter frame with the photograph she took last summer.

"You two are the couple," she says.

Paddy sets his mail back on the counter and comes over and stands next to Norine. He glances down at the picture in her hands, and from the clutter on the bench he absentmindedly takes up one of the fingerless neoprene gloves that Emily had sent with the picture, a Christmas package that arrived two days late. Day twenty-seven. He tugs the glove onto his right hand and, using his sleeved fingers, picks through the other tokens that had arrived in the package: a bottle of Gink, a pair of fold-up scissors, a "Rite in the Rain" notepad, a plastic

175

contraption with blinking red lights that affixes to the brim of a base-ball cap. He walks back to the counter, then back again to Norine's side, accepting the fact that he would be impossible to shop for. What else did you give a fifty-two year old fishing guide who owns every-thing he can possibly need—and who wants nothing more, it seems, than those things he uses, day after day, on the water?

"It was nice of her to send this," says Norine, replacing the photo on the bench. She looks at Paddy, and he feels his chest tighten and a sudden spasm of grief that feels utterly reckless. "Even if she's not available," adds Norine.

Norine steps away from Paddy and stands looking out the win-dow. He follows her gaze toward the ragged fringe of sky dressed all in gray. Nothing's moved, he thinks. No wind; no rain; the barometer tipping but a tap or two left or right; the temperature rising and fall-ing no more than a couple of degrees whether night or day. A storm of stagnation, decides Paddy, the leaden clouds having arrived New Year's Day, day thirty-two, halfway through his annual two-month retreat from guiding. December; January. Thirty-one days off the end of the year; thirty-one off the start of the next. Symmetry—as well as the shortest, harshest days of the year, when the effort it takes to find steelhead seems best reserved for his own solitary sport. Or, this year, he had hoped, almost no fishing at all, but instead the warmth and quiet of days spent systematically replenishing a season's store of flies, tying daylight hours in anticipation of long nights spent with Emily—

"I'm making tea. You want some?"

Norine moves past Paddy and is almost to the bottom of the stairs leading from both the basement and garage to the main floor before he emerges from his thoughts. She tugs off her scarf, hangs it from the headband and mail in her hand, waiting for his answer.

"Where's Fritz?"

"An away game. They win tonight they're in the playoffs."

Norine runs her free hand through her hair, a nut color—or maybe it's nutmeg—that Paddy's pretty sure comes mostly out of a bottle. Norine's not that young—although like most women he finds attractive these days, she looks a lot younger than he is.

"She'll call when she's ready," says Norine, turning to head upstairs. "Or email. Or not."

Paddy watches as Norine, starting up the stairs, wraps the scarf around her hand. As soon as she's out of sight, he hears a thump from the stairwell as if she punched the wall.

"I'm making you that tea," calls back Norine.

"Thanks," says Paddy.

He remains downstairs, his hovel of patience, perdition, uninterrupted desire. He goes to the counter and flips through his mail again then recrosses the room and checks his email, his phone messages, the weather. He sits down once more in front of his tying bench. His docket—a bound accounting journal, pages numbered, with columns he's indicated to show what patterns he intends to tie, what sizes and how many dozen of each—stares back at him, the lack of check marks and completion dates incriminating him with indolence.

Restraining himself this time, Paddy stares across the bench without reaching for the tiny picture of him and Emily that Norine took over the Fourth of July, a trip the three of them shared during the week off he schedules each year in the middle of his ten-month season. Symmetry. Even in his disconsolate state of mind, he recognizes how fortunate he is to have Norine in his life, a confidante since before his guiding career and through the entire run-up to Emily—a period of his life during which Paddy felt particularly adept at making women happy by falling head-over-heels in love, giving each of them, the way he saw it, the profound pleasure of knowing she remained capable of breaking a man's heart.

Is Emily any different? For the last six months he's felt absolutely sure of it. After his most foolish romance of all, allowing himself to fall for a married woman who turned out not to have the slightest desire to leave her husband, despite pronounced indications otherwise, Paddy rose from his despair in a state of numbness, only to receive from Norine irrefutable encouragement to venture online to see what he might find. He felt degraded by the whole process of profiling himself for inspection by complete strangers, a matter he found far more difficult than meeting new clients on the water, where, though at times still nervous, he was able to fall into the familiar rhythms of commanding his drift boat and practicing his angling craft to win over his charges. Yet when he described himself as an "independent fly fishing guide, about fifty, frank, funny, fit as a fireman and fun as a firecracker" and posted a picture of himself beneath fall colors alongside a favorite run while cradling a steelhead like a two-year-old in his arms, the response proved overwhelming. He had women coming at him from all directions. Norine sat back and watched him flounder through the thick of it, stepping in only to advise him to keep his cool for once, hold back, stay detached, take it easy. After a flurry of spring dates with Emily, however, during the up-and-down trout fishing prior to the salmonfly hatch, he felt the irresistible itch of love, against which he remained as defenseless as a teenager. With all due regard for Norine's caution and feminine advice, he kept his feelings to himself—until one evening he gave in to his lowest impulses and went upstairs and asked her about a "make-out spot"—somewhere she might know of since she and Fritz had raised three children and lived in the valley since coming to teach at the high school as newlyweds.

"A make-out spot?"

"Yeah. You know. Some place to park."

Norine, seated in her favorite chair, bare legs folded beneath her to one side, set her Patagonia catalog on the overstuffed armrest and took a drink from a bottle of Budweiser standing on the carpet.

"Well, there's the viewpoint. But you're liable to run into some of your ex-students."

Uneasy already about the nature of his request, Paddy began pacing the room.

"Who is this, anyway?" asked Norine. "The science teacher from Troutdale?"

"No. She thought "independent" meant independently wealthy."

"The engineer from White Salmon?"

Paddy shook his head.

"Turns out she's building this pyramid scheme based on serrated knives."

"The artist from The Dalles?

"Framed prints of classic works by the masters," quoted Paddy. "She pronounced Gauguin as if it rhymed with raging. Thought the Chinese printer must have left off the final G."

Paddy stops in the middle of the living room and looks directly at Norine.

"Then I mentioned casting for bonefish and getting distracted by a topless Tahitian. And that was that."

Norine sighed, swung her feet to the carpet and went to the kitchen. She came back with another bottle of beer.

"I told you—no jokes or innuendos until you actually meet face to face. Too many women can't read in anything funny when they see certain words in print."

"Tits?" asked Paddy.

"Tits," said Norine. She returned to her chair and took a long drink of beer. "So who is it you hope to park and make out with? The bimbo from Beulah?"

Before Paddy could answer, Norine stood up again and went to the front window. She moved the edge of the drapes aside and peered out into a breezy April night.

"Jesus, Paddy. Get yourself a goddamn motel room. Or bring her here, for Christ's sake."

Norine let the drapes fall shut and returned again to her chair while Paddy explained that he and Emily, Emily Thatcher from Beaverton, philosophy instructor and scholar in residence at the Rock Creek campus of Portland Community College, were a ways away from needing a motel room. What he didn't tell her, however, was that he couldn't envision bringing Emily or any other woman into Norine and Fritz's house for a night of lovemaking, that the thought of pitching about in frenzied embrace within calling distance and resonant contact with his two old teaching buddies and current housemates left him feeling uneasy for reasons he couldn't quite articulate and certainly didn't want to discuss. Norine, thank goodness, seemed unusually shortsighted about this odd streak of modesty, and she eventually revealed a secret spot that she and Fritz had enjoyed to frequent advantage during the busy decade when their house often felt overrun by needy children.

"And tell your psychic in residence she should bring binoculars and a star guide," added Norine. "Fritz and I used to get a sitter and a six-pack and say we were going to the movies. We'd put our beach chairs in the bed of the pickup and just relish the quiet."

Norine took another drink of beer and turned toward the window as if looking outside.

"That's an astronomy book, by the way—not astrology."

"Where is Fritz, anyway?" asked Paddy.

"Baseball. At Gresham. Playoffs in a couple of weeks."

As it turned out, the public picnic area behind the ranger station, coupled with a brand-new blow-up camp bed squeezed into the back of Paddy's twelve-year-old Suburban, proved perfectly adequate for

the next phase of courtship. Emily was a good sport about such hum-
ble appointments; she seemed genuinely tickled by the adventure of
nosing into the lot without aid of headlights, parking at the edge of
the forest, and climbing into the back to abandon herself to Paddy's
fervent advances. Up to a point. For no matter how much he tried
to interest her otherwise, Emily did want to stargaze, she did want
to hear about Paddy's guiding adventures, and she did want to talk
about what is real, what is good, and the point of their infinitesimal
lives.

And she didn't want to go all the way.

"What's with these women," complained Paddy, accepting a
Budweiser from Norine, "who just want friendship and no sex?"

"Give it a rest, big guy." With the school year finished, Norine
spent most of her time exercising and gardening, especially with Fritz
running clinics and sports camps for elementary kids and middle
schoolers throughout the valley. More often than not, she showed
up downstairs shortly after Paddy arrived home, finished showering
and, except for his recent once-a-week dates with Emily, sat down to
tie flies or phone or email clients. "You talk like that and your psychic
in residence is psychic gone AWOL."

Norine opened the slider leading out onto the tiny back deck,
releasing stale air trapped in the studio throughout another warm
June afternoon. Paddy, at his bench, reached for materials stirred to
life by the draft.

"It's not like we're goddamn kids," he said, snatching a feather
out of midair as it rocked slowly downward toward his moccasined
foot.

"All the more reason you should behave like adults."

Outside, Norine began deadheading peonies she had planted
that spring, part of a new perennial border she was creating, she said,
so that neighbors didn't have to look at the gear Paddy had started
storing there since emptying out the back of his Suburban. Bent over

in nylon running shorts, Norine revealed a view of her bottom and trim thighs that reminded Paddy of a moment during his last date, while Emily, on her knees, searched through her handbag for what he hoped might be some sort of lubricant but turned out to be only ChapStick—for her lips, she explained, because of so much kissing, a gentle rebuke that deflated Paddy's breathless anticipation and left him dizzy with frustration and, the next morning, sullen as a zombie until his client began sticking fish with a little Diving Caddis swung through a riffle beneath a faultless June sky.

"Adults get horny, too," he said, glimpsing, over the top of his tying glasses, the armload of wilted flowers as Norine moved about behind the gauzy screen of the slider.

"Oh, really," said Norine—and Paddy felt as if he had just told her that rivers run downhill.

Norine stopped while passing through the room on her way to the compost bins beyond the garage. With the back of her free arm she swiped at the sweat on her face, avoiding touching herself with her soiled fingers and hand.

"Too bad you can't use any of this for flies."

She raised the bundle of dead blossoms as if shrugging one shoulder.

"I guess plants are too fragile—or maybe predators only want flies made from parts of other animals. You ever ask the psychic about that?" she added.

Paddy didn't answer. When Norine returned, she carried a fresh bottle of beer from the refrigerator she and Fritz kept stocked in the garage. It occurred to him that she had been drinking since before he arrived home, a possibility that seemed even more likely when she started to pester him about any plans he might be making with Emily for his upcoming break over the Fourth of July.

"You better make it good," said Norine, gesturing with the bottle, held by the neck as if the handle of a dagger she was about to plunge into the headrest of his secondhand recliner. "I can guarantee you you're not going to get any farther rolling around in the back of your shaggin' wagon. You don't need a psychic to see that."

Paddy did have plans all right—but he was reluctant to share them. Norine's close tabs on his progress with Emily remained shaded by her stern advice to proceed slowly, the rather severe assessment that his failures in the past were due entirely to his hyped-up, overzealous nature, his eagerness to plunge into romance, to expose his feelings and the workings of his heart. If he really liked Emily, claimed Norine, if he really hoped to establish grounds for a lasting relationship and wanted something more than a playmate for exercise on the upgraded flotation device she sure as hell hoped he had written off as a business expense—if he was serious about her, argued Norine, he would do everything in his power to let Emily know that what he cared most about was spending time with her, whether they ever got around to sex or not.

Which was precisely why he sensed he should keep his plans—at least the details and intent of them—to himself. Feigning interest in the No-Name Soft-Hackle he had started before Norine arrived, he felt the weight of his subterfuge pull him off balance. What was the big deal? Despite Norine's cautionary tone, he merely hoped to establish a certain precedence before embarking on an extended vacation with Emily, so that neither of them had to expend any undue energy on a matter that seemed to him an inevitable consequence of their deepening intimacy.

God, he hated the need for this sort of obeisant rationale.

"What's that?" asked Norine, stretched out on the recliner.

"Eastern Oregon," offered Paddy vaguely. "We're going to head to Joseph. The Wallowas. There's a lot of small water where it'll be easy for Emily to catch—"

"The Zumwalt Prairie," said Norine, cutting Paddy short. She rocked the recliner upright, launching herself from the seat as if pitched from a boat brought too abruptly to the bank. "The Zumwalt Prairie," she said again—this time as though it were the name of a favorite singer or film—and by the time she finished speaking, she was close enough to Paddy to touch him.

Or strike him across the side of the head.

"Where's that?" he asked.

"Where's that?" repeated Norine—and to Paddy it suddenly seemed as if his old friend might have been drinking since breakfast, not only all afternoon.

"Where you been, big guy?"

A blanket of snow that mocks Paddy's fitful sleep confronts him as he approaches his computer before dawn of the forty-fourth day. He stands in the dark and through the narrow window gazes out at the still neighborhood, acknowledging the perverse irony of the white, unblemished street and the fervent dreams that left him panting by the time he wrestled himself awake. He recalls the lines of a Rilke poem from a collection Norine gave him for Christmas, the source of any number of grave or at least cryptic quotations he's included in missives to Emily in hopes that they might inspire a response, a tactic that suddenly strikes him as about as subtle as trying to fool a fish with a fly. *The storm, the shifter of shapes, drives on / across the woods and across time, / and the world looks as if it had no age.* This world, notes Paddy, appears anything but timeless—the houses, the parked cars, the naked, well-spaced trees all of a sort—yet the hour itself might belong to any part of the night, an idea that seems to him immediately ridiculed by the digital clock on his screen saver.

Yet for all his sour intimations, things do feel different this morning. As he sits down and touches the mouse, nudging the screen to life, Paddy mulls over the probability that this sense of change, of things having shifted, reflects but the obvious turn of weather, the same sharp fall of the barometer that has finally upended two weeks of stagnation and which he, like anglers everywhere, has always believed can trigger the best fishing. Yet when he tries to connect to the Internet, and he discovers he can't get online, he experiences a feeling of hollowness in a tiny spot that seems at the very center of the circumference described by the waistline of his Levi's, a feeling so strong it startles him and which he finds impossible to separate from sensations of hope and sensations of dread.

Still, there's a chance that Fritz and Norine's DSL connection, unlike his cheap dial-up service, remains live. He tidies up his tying bench until he hears the two of them stirring upstairs. Then it occurs to Paddy that schools might be closed or at least delayed; he should give them a chance to spend the time alone. He busies himself with a shower, breakfast, a second pot of coffee, the serious puttering of a genuine bench cleaning—until he hears Fritz's pickup start up and drive away.

He carries his coffee upstairs and finds Norine in the kitchen in her bathrobe, her hair wrapped in a towel. While he explains his computer problem, she goes to the cupboard above the refrigerator and takes down the bottle of single-malt he bought her and Fritz for Christmas and pours a rip into her coffee.

"No school?" asks Paddy.

"Two-hour delay."

Norine gestures with the bottle, inviting Paddy to join her. He places a hand over his cup.

"You don't worry about someone saying something?"

"I'm the health teacher," says Norine. "Who's going to notice?"

Bottle in hand, she raises her arms and strikes a body-builder pose, pretending to flex her biceps.

"Where'd Fritz go?"

Norine returns the bottle to the cupboard. "He's worried they're going to cancel afternoon practices." She removes the towel from her

185

head and shakes out her hair. "He's been up all morning calling his players, trying to schedule something this morning."

"They must have won last night."

"They must have," agrees Norine.

Paddy brings up his Internet problem again. He waits in the kitchen while Norine goes to the bedroom to get her laptop, returning in a pair of school warm-ups, the teaching outfit she favors over the need to keep up with the latest fashions. She sets the laptop on the kitchen counter next to the phone but leaves a hand resting on the lid.

"You know you maybe ought to give it a rest," she says. "It's not like these emails are getting you anywhere."

Paddy looks at Norine while she finishes her last swallow of coffee. Then he turns to the window above the sink as a car leaves another set of tracks in the street.

"Yeah?" he says.

"Obviously something made her skittish. You guys were going pretty hot and heavy there for awhile."

"Isn't that the point?"

Paddy turns back and faces Norine.

"Maybe. I don't know." Norine goes to the back entry off the kitchen and brings back a pair of Sorels. She pulls the boots on over her stockinged feet and stuffs in her pantlegs and begins tightening the laces. "I think maybe you're just pestering her now—like when you keep on casting to a fish you can't get to rise. Eventually you just have to stop and let things settle down for awhile. Be patient. Let her get comfortable again."

"When did you become the expert?"

"About what? Fish or women?" Norine stands up straight and runs her hands through her hair. "Or love."

186

Norine digs through a book bag on the counter and produces a tube of something she applies to her lips. She turns to Paddy and makes a kissing gesture with her mouth.

"How do I look?"

"Like a half-drunk slut."

"Perfect. 'Long as I can still intimidate the freshmen boys."

Yet as soon as Norine leaves for school and Paddy sits down at his bench to begin tying flies, he picks up the picture of him and Emily and spins around to his computer and tries to get online. No dice. He considers going upstairs to use Norine's laptop then decides maybe she's right, maybe he has made Emily nervous as though putting down a trout and he just needs to stop casting for awhile. What would he say, anyway? He opens the collection of poetry titled *Risking Everything* that he's been pulling quotes out of and turns to pages he's dated so he doesn't forget and repeat lines. 12/30: *Anything or anyone that does not bring you alive is too small for you.* 1/4: *So, when the shoe fits/The foot is forgotten,/When the belt fits/The belly is forgotten,/When the heart is right/"For" and "against" are forgotten.* And his favorite, by that old madman Rumi, 1/10: *Let the beauty we love be what we do./There are hundreds of ways to kneel and kiss the ground.* Paddy tries to imagine Emily reading this stuff, tries to get inside her agile mind and hear how it sounds to her—and he quickly comes to the conclusion that it all sounds the same: "I love you! Let's fuck some more!" In a fit of self-loathing he considers the possibility that his oft-professed emotional availability might in fact be nothing more than juvenile badgering, as strident as a sophomore's plea for attention. Or a client's demand for another steelhead after one that got away. Maybe what he calls sharing his emotions is just a kind of whip to try to force women into bed.

This troubling view of himself revives the sensation of hollowness in the pit of his stomach; Paddy turns back to his bench, determined to stop moping and start producing flies. With over two weeks ahead of him, he still has time to salvage his so-called off season—if he can get serious. Again he picks up the picture of him and Emily, and he studies it one last time, examining her easy smile, the athletic slope of her shoulders, the shadows highlighting the curve of the T-shirt concealing her piquant breasts—all of it captured against the backdrop of the remote prairie while Norine invited them to show the camera the feelings stirring inside their hearts.

Yet it still seems odd to Paddy, even at this late date, even after all of the fun the three of them have shared, that Emily agreed to allow Norine to accompany them that week in the first place. He recalls lying with Emily in his arms late in the week following a stint of particularly demonstrative lovemaking and, under a spell of gratitude during which he's allowed, throughout his life, any number of unguarded comments to slip from his mouth, he asked her straight out why she had agreed to let Norine tag along. Emily, wriggling her backside into him, offered up the sort of profound, guileless reasoning that he was only then getting used to, claiming "it just seemed to make sense."

"And look how it turned out," she added, aligning her fanny such that Paddy felt their little tent and air bed was about to be reduced—Alice-like—to a new, unfathomable dimension. "We're already practically the best of friends."

Norine's presence hardly seemed the most pressing concern. She had brought her own tent, and she kept it positioned throughout the trip at a distance as discreet as space allowed. A friend of hers from Joseph who worked for The Nature Conservancy provided overnight access to the prairie, and when Paddy and Emily decided to set up camp at the edge of a seductive pine copse halfway up the flank of one of the Findley Buttes, Norine chose to spend the night alone "up with the stars and the last of the wildflowers" near the cairn from which, earlier that day, they had studied the lay of the land, in all directions, from the Wallowas to the Blue Mountains to the precarious ridgelines pitched in furious descent toward the floor of Hells Canyon.

Even when they all decided to spend a night on the town in Joseph, Norine was quick to take a separate room—an arrangement that seemed perfectly natural until Paddy ended up in her bed.

He is sure he was innocent of any crime. The next morning the three of them laughed at his failure to hold his liquor, the Cuervo Gold Norine first produced at the end of a vigorous hike up the west fork of the Wallowa River above Wallowa Lake, a climb through the quiet heat of a July morning that left them gritty with sweat and dust, unable to resist the invitation of a shaded pool at the edge of the Six-Mile Meadow. The water, clear as the tequila they took shots of while pulling off their shoes and socks, seemed fused from the granite substrate lining the pool, the perfect transparency tinted as if the palest gemstone where the stream-sized fork, in a moment of remission, rested before pitching headlong into the steep forest. By the time they all had removed most of their clothing, Paddy felt the mild euphoria of alcohol stirred into the heat, the exercise, the altitude and spontaneous blur of naked flesh. He headed directly for the water, conscious of his excited state, and as he slipped through the surface the shock of the cold felt as close to flame as to ice.

Yet when the rush of immersion subsided, only he and Norine stood naked in the pool. Emily, her back to them in the shade atop the bank, was pulling her T-shirt over her head, her fair bottom already clad in plain, French-cut briefs. Paddy felt suddenly exposed by his own reckless plunge—and he kept his eyes off Norine and edged away from her as if some unidentifiable substance had just floated to the surface of the pool.

It was the tequila, he would later claim, that was the source of these silly antics that continued throughout the day and into the night and found him, the next morning, in Norine's bed. By himself, thank God. The bottle, Paddy recalls, dropping another Wild

189

Hare into an open Altoids tin next to his vise, seemed to hover about them as they careened off the mountain and back into town, from bar to bar, from karaoke stage to dance floor, as if a comet trapped in the gravity of their reckless orbit. There was probably a second bottle, he suspects. Maybe a third. And it's the memory of this night of debauchery that now opens the hollow spot in his stomach and fills it with dread, a sensation that has haunted him, again and again, throughout the past forty-four days of unanswered mail.

∽

He ties on into the afternoon, stopping only to refresh his coffee, fix a quesadilla, and pause now and then to gaze out at the snow and submit to his pitiful heartache. He finds it contemptible that he might have already lost someone he longs for so intently. All day he resists the urge to see if he's able to get online and check his email. He ties, instead, with the steadfast indignation of his working-class roots, savoring the bitterness of his own misguided life.

He quits only after counting the flies and, finding himself two short of an even five dozen, quickly tying two more. He records the total in his docket, trying to convince himself that it's a start—certainly a hell of a lot better than he's been doing. He turns to his computer and finds he's still unable to get online. He goes upstairs to see what he can find out there.

It's just like Norine to have passwords on a piece of scratch paper taped to the screen of her laptop. Her browser opens automatically to an iGoogle page. Paddy tries logging into his gmail account, finally remembering a password that works. He never uses the account anyway. He can't recall if Emily even has the address.

But when he returns to Norine's iGoogle page, and he sees she has a message, he clicks on it and, to his surprise, he's into her gmail account and the message is from "Psychnres."

It takes Paddy all of a couple of minutes to discover that Norine and Emily have been emailing one another steadily for the last two months. And when Norine comes up the stairs, having passed through his place to drop off his mail, she sees immediately what's up and she stops and looks at him and shakes her head.

"You shouldn't read other people's mail," she says.

She goes directly to the bottle of single-malt. She drops ice cubes into a pair of glasses, fills them both with Scotch and, bottle in hand, heads downstairs. Paddy follows. Across the room from each other they sip their drinks in silence, Paddy believing he's too numb to speak. But soon the Scotch insists he's not numb at all, and when Norine walks over and embraces him, he feels absolutely alive.

At one point she tells him that Fritz is gone for the night, in Bend to scout a probable playoff opponent. Later, in his bed, Norine tries to convince him that nothing has changed, all this means is that they've shared an evening of fun.

"If anything had been different," she says, her face aligned perfectly above his, "everything would be different now. I wouldn't feel like I feel. You'd feel differently, too. You don't need a philosopher to explain that."

He doesn't buy it for a second. At the same time, he feels powerless to fashion an argument. Once, during the middle of the night, while Norine sleeps soundly at his side, he follows a long stream of reason that seems to explain clearly why he finds himself exactly where he is at this moment in his life, how it is he failed Emily by offering her emotions that deprived her of the excitement she might have gleaned had she been forced to fish for them, little by little, instead of having them land in her lap all at once, the power over him she would have felt had she called forth, cast after cast, that part of him he had so willingly given.

But in the morning, Paddy's only able to articulate a single, simple thought.

## Lost in Wyoming

"Everything *has* changed," he tells Norine.
"You're probably right," she agrees.